A CREATURE OF SPIRIT

The Trouble with Mollie - Book Three

RAFFAELLA ROWELL

Published by Blushing Books
An Imprint of
ABCD Graphics and Design, Inc.
A Virginia Corporation
977 Seminole Trail #233
Charlottesville, VA 22901

Raffaella Rowell
A Creature of Spirit

eBook ISBN: 978-1-63954-093-8
Print ISBN: 978-1-63954-094-5
v2

Chapter 1

Mollie Sorensen was on a high and surveyed the dancers, thrilled. She felt triumphant. Her party was a great success. She tapped her foot to the beat of the music and waved her hand in salute to a friend in demonstrative cheerfulness, beaming with delight.

The party was in full swing on that Saturday night. The orchestra played on a podium in the stylish white marquee, on the large grounds of her Oxford home. It had been blazing its flamboyant music and pulsating its rhythms for the last three hours, from rumba to salsa and everything in-between. Everybody danced merrily under the quaint, colourful fairy lights hanging loose in the marquee and in the gardens. Thus, giving the party a warm glow and a fairytale vibe to it.

Her guests, in all their finery, looked like a picture in their elegant evening wear. Their dancing feet, on overdrive, were swinging to the tunes. The mood was vibrant; they were having a blast.

It was late August. The night was unfolding under a splendid starlit sky, with millions of stars beaming their silvery, mystical twinkles. A cool summer breeze gave everyone a truce from the heat of the season and the dance.

Food and drink were plentiful. She had set a cold and hot buffet up at the other end of the large marquee. Small tables gathered in its proximity for guests to rest and to have a bite in comfort.

She glanced at the couples twirling on the dance floor. Her eyes caught Fergus and Marguerite swaying sexily; any closer, the two would meld into one person.

I have done that, Mollie sighed, satisfied. She had a helping hand in matching that union.

She felt proud of herself for seeing them so cozy. If she had not followed her instinct, they would not be together, let alone be deliriously happy. The powerful Earl of Buckley himself, now a few months into the marriage, had given her a tender smile and ruffled her hair tonight. It was a testament to Fergus's contentment with his bride.

A satisfied grin formed on Mollie's lips, watching them so wrapped up in each other. It'd been a huge tick in the box for the dating app, not to mention she was ecstatic at their happiness after the bumpy start.

Her eyes moved on, and they landed on Finley and Kathryn as they twirled to the music, too. They were her special guests, whose official engagement they celebrated that night. The party was held in their honour; her friends got engaged a few months back, and she wished to do something special for them.

I did that too, she thought with a well-pleased glint in her eyes. Her best friend, Kathryn, had pined for Finley for almost a year, and if she had not given the man a push, the poor girl would still be waiting for the fellow to make a move. They were to set a wedding date soon. He could not wait to marry his girl, to make her his wife.

Mollie gave out a gigantic sigh of pleasure, purring like a cat. She grinned from ear to ear, gratified. She felt elated seeing people in love.

Her eyes darted to Erin Blake next, and her heart sank! A forceful hiss of irritation left her mouth instead.

Mollie muttered an oath under her breath when she saw her friend sitting at a table at the other end of the marque. The woman had a soft drink in her hands, twirling it incessantly; she cut an odd, peculiar figure amongst the merriment, looking prim and wooden, despite her pretty demeanour.

Mollie had undertaken every effort to get her to the party.

Erin was tall and slender, a stunning brunette. But she was shy and rather awkward for someone so pretty, an introvert, but then she had a lot of issues. That night, to her hostess's bewilderment, Erin kept refusing every man who asked her to dance. Mollie rolled her eyes. She wished her friend relaxed, had fun, and enjoyed the festivities instead.

She had insisted with Dr. Stewart to give Erin his consent to leave the clinic to attend the party. It was only for a weekend, but it took her an entire month of insistence and begging before the doctor granted his permission. Erin was convalescing in his clinic, and he worried it may be too soon. Of course, the doctor had been invited too.

So, the previous day, Erin had set out by train to Oxford, but to persuade him to allow her to travel alone had been another palaver, the doctor not convinced she was ready for this, either. But Mollie was determined to get her way. Thus, he relented and allowed Erin to go ahead.

The busy doctor had only just arrived in time for the party instead. The plan was for them to stay in her home until Monday morning, when they would return together to the clinic.

Dr. Stewart spent most of the evening talking to Zac, Finley, Alex, and Fergus in turn.

Though, Mollie noticed, he kept giving furtive glances at Erin when he thought no one was looking. She wasn't sure if it was because Erin was a patient at his clinic and he wanted to keep an eye on her or if there was more to it. The doctor had not directed a single word to the girl since his arrival, though, which she found strange.

Could it be? Dr. Stewart fancied Erin? And she? Who knew?

Um…

She wasn't sure what to make of them. Was Erin well enough? Perhaps! This was a difficult situation, uncharted territory for her.

Erin had been in the clinic for four months now, and to all accounts, she was on the mend. Mollie and Kathryn had visited her often there, and in that time, despite their troubled past, a solid friendship had developed between the three girls.

Their distressful past put aside, it was forgiven and forgotten. It had been rather purging for the three women to do this. And once they crossed the first few awkward visits, a positive understanding replaced the tumultuous and complex past between them instead. A friendship had blossomed.

So, that night, it pained Mollie to see her friend like this, cutting a sad figure amid a cheerful party.

Nothing I can do about it, she thought with a heavy sigh. Or could she? She liked a challenge; she relished them. She was pensive for a while. Though Erin and Dr. Stewart were a puzzle to her, both so reserved, so restrained.

Mollie had to be careful. Dr. Stewart was an eminent doctor, older than most of her friends, and too serious. She didn't know him that well; he was Zac's friend.

She groaned. A booming roar reached her ears from the dance floor, distracting her, *George!* She recognised his bass, sonorous laugh. She spun to him and grinned. His roaring laugh was contagious. It echoed over the loud music in the marquee. She observed him.

George and Imelda, another puzzle. They were swinging and swaying their hips, their eyes locked on one another. They so obviously cared for each other. Undeniable! She felt the sexy heat emanating from them as they danced. She smiled.

Look at them. The way they flirted was wonderful to watch. Yes, she was right. But as she studied her young friends, she mused about them too. They were not a couple yet, why?

I must talk to Imelda on this, one of these days, but she is not my priority tonight. She can look after herself. First things first…

That evening, Mollie decided she had other priorities. *Why can't Erin flirt with Dr. Stewart, like Imelda flirts with George?* She was sure sparks would fly, if only the woman would let herself go. She contemplated her conundrum, but she was at a loss.

"Zac, darling," Mollie beamed at her husband when she felt his arm circle around her waistline, thus interrupting her musings.

"Hey, what are you doing here in the corner watching everyone? Umm... You look like a queen studying her subjects." Zac struggled to be heard over the hubbub of the party as she followed the motion of his lips to match the words. He gave her a peck on the lips and taking her, he encouraged her to follow him out of the marquee into the garden where the music was not so loud.

"Are you enjoying tonight?" she asked.

"A wonderful party, you've done a great job. Kat and Finley are thrilled with the celebration."

"Aha! A beautiful couple. So happy, aren't they?" she mumbled, but she was a little distracted as they stopped and she looked back.

"Who are you staring at, ah?" Zac scoffed, trying to see who was absorbing his wife's attention. Mollie was still glancing towards the marquee through the open sides.

"Do you think Dr. Stewart likes Erin?"

"What?" Her husband wondered what she was on about now.

"You heard me. He keeps looking at her. Is he doing it because she is under his care, because he is her doctor, or is there something else? You know him best. What do you think?"

"Well, I guess so, she is in his care. You are not planning something, are you?"

"Me? No, of course not." *We'll see, umm… who knows? They are staying the weekend after all, and Erin is my priority.*

"I told you, Mollie, you mustn't meddle with people."

"I am not doing anything, Zac. I am observing, that's all."

"Exactly what I am afraid of."

"Don't be silly!"

"Now, dance with me!" He took her by the elbow, trying to move her along.

"Yes, I will. In a minute. Hold on, the doctor is in the garden, and Erin is at the table, alone…" And she was off instead in an instant, doing her own bidding.

"Where are you going—" her husband huffed and rolled his eyes.

Mollie moved towards the doctor, strolling in the grounds.

"Dr. Stewart, are you enjoying yourself?" She gave him her most welcoming smile, and with her baby blue eyes wide, she looked innocent and cute.

"Lovely party, Mollie. Thank you for inviting me. Please, call me Marcus," Dr. Stewart said with a courteous nod of the head.

"Come, Marcus, you must dance. We don't want any lovely young ladies to be a wallflower at my party, do we?"

"I beg your pardon?"

"Erin!"

"Ah?"

"You must dance with her. She's been twirling that soft drink in her hands all night. Please, ask her to dance, man," Mollie urged with a childish grin that was difficult to oppose. She took him by the elbow and steered him back towards the marque.

"What is my girl asking you to do, Marcus?" Zac intercepted them. He raised an eyebrow to his wife, seeing a worried expression on his friend's face.

"Just asking him to dance with Erin, that's all," Mollie countered in all virtuosity, "Not a taxing request, is it? Look at her; she is so pretty," she concluded with her baby blue eyes so wide pleading with Marcus, and a little sweet pout formed on her lips.

"But he is her doctor," Zac replied with concern, and his body stood firm in front of them to stop their advance.

"Well, no... strictly speaking, I'm not," Dr. Stewart said. "Miss Blake is in my clinic, yes, but she is Dr. Devlin's patient. Julia is her doctor, not me. So, nothing wrong with me dancing with her," he went on and coughed, somewhat self-conscious at his own admission.

"See? I told you so!" Mollie launched a smile at her husband. "Then go, Marcus. Erin's been sitting there for ages. No one asked her to dance all night," she lied. "Go save the day."

Dr. Stewart had been observant. He raised an elegant brow at his hostess, knowing full well the stunning brunette had had a string of fellows asking her for a dance, but no one seemed to have satisfied her enough to accept.

Mollie bumped him with her shoulder on his chest, encouraging him to go. She waved her hands, shooing him off while he made his way to Erin.

She stood there. She watched Marcus approach the woman, and she was only satisfied when he led Erin to the dance floor.

"Now, I can dance with you, darling!" Mollie smiled, turning to her husband with a love-struck expression.

"You are impossible, babe," Zac scoffed with a shake of his head, an amused twinkle in his eyes.

^b

Chapter 2

As Marcus invited Erin to dance, his mind could not help but drift to when she arrived at his clinic. As he circled her waist and held her hand to sway to the music, his thoughts went back to that first morning four months ago, when he laid eyes on Erin Blake again after so long.

That day he had grown impatient. He was in his office waiting for her. "Stevenson," he barked, "find Miss Blake, please, and bring her to me. She's late for her appointment," Dr. Stewart commanded the young nurse to look for the woman.

The silly wretch was half an hour late, he remembered.

He was on tenterhooks in more ways than one, eager to meet with her. Marcus fidgeted with the lamp on his desk. He lit it, then realising it was morning, he turned it off. He fretted with a family photo, adjusting its position on the counter, and some papers, too. Aware he was just tampering with things remarkably out of character for him, he straightened up, pulled his shoulders backwards and inhaled. Why was his heartbeat racing?

He paced the room. His own behaviour confused him. Miss Blake's lateness irritated him. He shifted towards the window; he held his arms behind his back, pensive, staring out onto the lawn.

Then, he saw her. A tall, slender, striking brunette was aimlessly strolling in his gardens. He knew everybody in his clinic, and he had not seen this woman yet. *It must be her!* And a memory of long ago resurfaced in his mind. He had a glimpse at the face of the woman for an instant. *Could it be her?*

Something called his attention back and out of his reverie. A door slammed somewhere in the hallway. He remembered having seen the glass doors to the grounds in the waiting room left open. He cursed under his breath at this distraction and at the sentimental memory resurfacing after so long. It had no place to be there. It irritated him. The minx on the lawn appeared to have no intention of meeting him as scheduled.

He watched the woman, following her every movement. She was oblivious to the world as she strolled leisurely in his garden, even though she knew she had an interview to keep.

Women!

He had back-to-back appointments. He ran his clinic in a busy atmosphere. A timetable full of patients to see, with all the peripherals of running a successful, large clinic on his shoulders. He planned his schedule with painstaking precision every week, with no margin for errors. A well-oiled military machine that ran with efficiency to exactitude, to perfection. His appointments had to run effortlessly to plan to fulfil them all, to provide everybody with their fair share of him. And she had wasted half an hour of his precious time.

He sighed and closed his eyes for a moment.

That day at his clinic, she perched on a bench in the garden. *Has she forgotten about the appointment? Bloody Hell, the lady will have to understand the rules!*

Marcus opened the floor-to-ceiling French doors in his office, stepped outside and walked to her. He halted next to her, as she sat on a bench with her face towards the blue limpid sky and her eyes closed.

"Miss Blake?" he called out at first softly, almost reverently. He recognised the large, almond-shaped black eyes in a second as she opened them. They were unmistakable.

"That's me," she said with a faint smile.

"You are late, Miss Blake! Get your lazy bottom off that bench. Now, please, and hurry to my office. On the double! I have no time to waste," he continued peremptorily and made his way back without a further word or glance to her.

THAT SAME DAY four months ago, as Erin sat on that bench in the sunshine with her eyes closed, a deep baritone, silvery voice, silky and modulated at first, melodically reached her ears. She smiled, as if she were in a sweet dream at the masculine, suave tone.

She opened her eyes and glanced up. The sun bothered her, so she squinted a few times to look at him in the bright light.

"That's me," she answered curiously, with the smile still on her lips, not knowing who this tall man standing in front of her was. Oh, but how she liked his voice pronouncing her name, so pleasant, so warming. Though his next commanding, harsh words jolted her out of her dreamy state.

She stood up jerkily and peered at the towering man retreating to his office, his massive shoulders and back to her.

Blast! She realised who the fellow was. *I forgot all about the rules-mongering doctor! Is that him? He didn't sound too pleased.*

She had lost track of time and forgotten all about having her first interview with him while she appreciated the beautiful lawns and amazing landscapes surrounding the clinic, deep in the Worcestershire countryside.

"Miss Blake! There you are," Nurse Stevenson said, running towards her in a huff, while Erin smoothed her dress with her hands.

"Hello, there."

"Good heavens, Miss Blake, Dr. Stewart has been expecting you. Where have you been? You are late! He does not like waiting," the nurse said, none too happy with her, either.

Erin sighed and closed her eyes. "That's where I'm going," she replied in mild panic, pointing at the man heading to the office and trying to hurry after him.

"Oh, he won't be pleased," Stevenson launched in a huff, shuffling after her.

Erin scurried along, entering the study after the fellow, followed by the nurse.

"Miss Blake is here, Doctor," the nurse mumbled, realising he was not in a sunny disposition when people made him wait.

"Thank you, I'll handle this," he said as the young woman nodded and left the room.

Erin peeked at her watch and rolled her eyes. Agitation took hold of her. She was late, nervous! Not knowing what to expect, she fiddled with the amethyst stone pendant at the centre of her necklace. She was fatigued because of the late-night arrival at the clinic. Erin had welcomed the few minutes of calm outside, but she was sure she would regret her lovely, sunny interlude. She was rather reserved, and she felt uncomfortable standing there in front of him. Perspiration erupted on her upper lip.

He closed the glass doors to the garden. He gave her a swift glance, from head to toe. Erin was a tall woman; there was a lot of her. He lingered on her face but said nothing. He was inscrutable.

She shuffled on her feet, hesitant, restless, as he seemed to inspect her. She was rather shy, and his unabashed stare made her feel ill at ease. Was he trying to establish control over her, power over her?

He motioned to the chair in front of him with a dismissive wave of his hand, and he sat behind his desk. "Miss Blake, this is your first day in my clinic. Let me tell you, this is a busy medical centre. You are half an hour late. Nurse Stevenson told you the exact time of our appointment, did she not? She warned you, I don't like lateness. Did she or did she not say this to you?"

"Y-yes," she stammered, and a red flush crept up her neck, her eyes downcast.

"I'll disregard your lateness today because you are new here. But I insist on punctuality. I won't accept this again. You must be on time to your appointments either with me, or with any of my staff. Do I make myself clear?"

"Yes, Doctor. I am sorry." She had no justification for her lateness. He found her sitting in the fresh air, with not a care in the world, on the magnificent lawns in the sunshine. She opted for silence.

He appeared to regard her curiously, and she had goosebumps at his implacable scrutiny.

"Umm... resting, were you?" he said sardonically. "I suppose you are tired from your late arrival last night," he went on, arching his eyebrows. His face had a deadpan expression, an impassiveness she couldn't read. For a fleeting second, she had seen a mischievous glint in his eyes.

"No, I-I..." she stuttered, but he put his hand up as if to say, *I don't need an answer to that!* And she blushed. His super-efficient business manner irritated her, not to mention his obvious inspection of her.

"Miss Blake, I was going to have a longer conversation with you, but given I have another appointment in less than ten minutes, we'll go straight to the point and forget the pleasantries."

"Pleasantries?" she asked, surprised, but he ignored her and went on.

"I have assigned you to Dr. Julia Devlin. She will ensure your well-being while you are with us, treat you, so that you can be well again in no time. Stevenson will conduct you to her right after this. You shall begin straight away. You'll sit daily periods with her, no lateness, please! Dr. Devlin is an outstanding doctor and she'll secure your improvement. You'll see me once or twice a week, to discuss progress or any question you may have. The nurse will give you the schedule in advance."

He kept talking about the sessions required, the treatment, with whom and how, and the purpose of them. He talked fast, to ensure he would say all the necessary in the short time remaining but other than Dr. Devlin's name, and a few other things, all Erin heard was blah blah, blah… instead, she had a good look at him.

If you are going to inspect me, like a specimen in a museum, then I can do it too, you know!

That suave voice had intrigued her, even though there was no sign of it at the moment. This time he was businesslike, firm, peremptory in his statements.

Erin was a tall woman; few men were taller than she was. When she was standing in front of him moments earlier, before they were sitting, she had to look up to him; the man towered over her. *Um…* now that was novel to her.

She couldn't pinpoint his age, *but he must be a few years older than me,* and she was thirty-three. Erin reckoned he was in his late thirties, perhaps he looked younger than he was? Who knew?

A tall, athletic man, he was dashing, with an attractive face with strong, manly features. Not to ignore the mighty body, and in that well-cut blue suit of his, it gave him a stylish bearing. He looked like a vintage, refined model rather than a doctor.

Did he remind her of somebody? Um… perhaps. There was something familiar about him. Yet, she was sure she had not seen him before, had she? No. She would remember someone like him, so handsome, surely! Wouldn't she? A handsome fellow who could have more than his fair share of women. Erin saw a ring on his finger, as he waved his hand in the air to emphasise a point he made. *Damn!* The ring glittered in the sunlight. Bloody hell! That meant there was a spouse somewhere. *Damn and double damn!*

He caught her staring at his hand, precisely at his ring. Even now, as a widower, Marcus never took his wedding ring off. It appeared offensive to the memory of his late wife.

Erin soon discovered this bit of news as the days went by. He was a widower, to her considerable relief, meaning he was a free man.

A slow grin curved up on his lips at her obvious attention of the ring, and at his smile, something happened to her.

The first time she had seen him smile that morning, and it felt like a cozy bear-hug.

Suddenly, something warmed between her legs as she watched his perfect fleshy lips produce a thick smile and move as he continued speaking. She wished she could pass her thumb over them, lick his lips with her tongue. She had been off sex for a long time.

The grief at losing her twin brother, then within months, losing her parents, had been tremendous. After the death of her family in such a brief space of time, she had gone off the rails, doing strange things to herself and to others, hence the necessity of her treatment in this clinic. Erin Blake hadn't even thought of sex, not even cared.

That first day, in Dr. Stewart's office, a steer down below, between her legs, made her clit throb. It was the second time in two consecutive days that Erin's libido had reminded her she still had a pussy, and her underused, almost forgotten, hot kitty was in urgent need of attention. Her desires stirred in her again, this time for Dr. Stewart! But this one was on a massive scale. Unparalleled in all her life! A nuclear explosion of lust burst in her body.

Her sexual desires awakened with a bang. As if the big bang that marked the origins of the universe was marking the origins of her lust for this man, now expanding uncontrollably within her frame.

Eight months without thinking of it; even before then, she had little sex since she ended the relationship with her fiancé two years ago.

A recurring thought… her vagina was growing cobwebs! She was convinced of it.

She was sure no man could make love to her again. Her passage must be clogged up with dust and cobwebs, like an abandoned and dilapidated old mine. That's what it felt to her. Any fellow would have to fight his way through debris accumulated through years of disuse. An unappealing thought to the opposite sex, she was sure!

Could a woman become a virgin again by not using her pussy? By not making love? Should she ask him? He was a doctor after all! she thought in amusement! She wondered what his answer would be. Would her question shock the man? Man? What man? Who was she kidding? This man was off limits to her. He was too good-looking and too distinguished to be interested in the likes of her, a sorrowful mess of a woman.

She smiled at her preposterous thoughts. This handsome doctor had resurfaced these long-lost passions in her belly, the giddiness that had left her long ago. *Oh, sweet Jesus,* so many seasons had passed since she had any action in that department. She was sure she'd forgotten how to do it, how to make love. How to even kiss a man!

A deep sigh escaped her involuntarily. Dr. Stewart studied her, and he halted his speech at her sigh. She blushed scarlet at her weird, horny thoughts while his eyes scrutinised her. She felt the sexual stir acutely down below, aware of the handsome man before her, and flushed as if she were a teenager. Again!

She must stop having this kind of horny thoughts when she glanced at a gorgeous fellow. It was embarrassing, out of character. In particular with a man so respectable and so prominent, like this doctor. He must think her an idiot!

"Are you okay, Miss Blake?" he asked, looking at her with great attention. He detected something in her eyes. The slow, involuntary release of breath coming out of her mouth, which she could not stop, caused a frown on his face. He must have guessed something.

She was mortified when his lips curled up on one side. She blushed to the root of her hair. She suddenly stood up and wrung her hands, ashamed of her lascivious musings.

"Are we finished, Doctor?" she asked, wanting to run away from his office as fast as she could.

"Sit down, Miss Blake, we'll finish when I say so." he rebuked, his expression harsh at having interrupted his flow, and pointed to the chair.

She raised her chin at him, and her eyes narrowed, contemplating rebellion despite the warmth between her legs.

The sudden, intense glare she got back from him made her gulp. It said to her, *do not even try it!*

"Please…" he added in a more conciliatory tone, pointing to her seat, and she plopped down on her chair.

But the conciliation didn't last long.

"Miss Blake, let me make something absolutely clear to you. This is your first day in my clinic. I'll overlook the poor behaviour for now. While you are in here, under my care, you'll abide by my rules. All of them! You missed breakfast this morning and I'll not have patients missing meals. I suggest you familiarise yourself with mealtimes and my rules. Here is a copy of them in case you misplaced them." He handed her a sheet of paper.

"How could I forget? They are pinned behind my bedroom door." She took the paper with the infamous rules.

"So, you have read them, I take it."

"No!"

He scowled at her, not pleased.

She wrung her hands, her eyes downcast. It was the wrong answer.

"I suggest you read them, and soon. And another thing, I will not have patients fraternising in their rooms with alcohol, as if they were at a party. Understood? This is not a university's halls." This time the rebuke was harsh.

She blanched. Bloody hell, this man knew everything! "Yes, I am sorry." Erin lowered her eyes, remembering she had drunk some wine upon her late arrival the night before. That was until the matron had seen the lights on in her room and discovered she was drinking. The woman had removed the offending items.

"You can go. Nurse Stevenson is outside; she will take you to Dr. Devlin. I'll see you next week. Good day, Miss Blake." Thus, he dismissed her.

THIS HAD BEEN their encounter at the clinic on her first day. Since then, Dr. Stewart and Erin met twice a week for fifteen minutes in his office for four months, to talk about her progress with the treatment.

From that first day onwards, though, their eyes always searched for the other. Furtive glances to one another were in order whenever they glimpsed at the other somewhere on the grounds. They couldn't help their attraction.

The doctor conducted the meetings in a prim and officious manner, giving nothing away, his duty to his work paramount. Despite his professional demeanour, waters ran deep. Once, beaming at her sweet face, he lost the train of conversation. He went on with a wistful tone, then coughed and recovered his composure soon enough.

On another occasion, they smiled at one another, their eyes locked with a visible yearning gleaming when Marcus caught her peering out of the window at him. But that was the extent of it.

Thus, four months had passed.

Yet there was a time long before this, which she seemed to be oblivious to. Erin had not remembered meeting him before then, and he had never reminded her about their encounter at the regatta years ago. He felt hurt she had not recognised him.

Why should she? His constant thought. She'd been with a boyfriend. There was no reason for noticing him.

Neither of them could deny that there was a powerful attraction between them now, even though they both tried to squash their emerging feelings. They would not act upon them, each for different reasons.

Chapter 3

Four months down the line, on the dance floor at Mollie's party with their bodies in such proximity, Erin's heartbeat was rising. It was drumming in her throat. She assumed Dr. Stewart could hear it; the beating was so loud to her own ears. If he were to gaze into her black pools, the inordinate shine in her eyes would tell him a story.

His arm circled her, and his big palm landed on the small of her back. He drew her to him, while the other wrapped around her much smaller hand.

The electric wave from his touch travelled across her frame and spread to her limbs at the speed of light. Her body trembled with dread and excitement mingled.

"Are you okay, Miss Blake?" he asked. His deep baritone, silky tone reached her while his lips brushed her ear.

"Y-yes, Dr. Stewart," she mumbled nervously. She sensed butterflies in her stomach, her breathing constricted. She was perspiring.

"Call me Marcus. We aren't at the clinic this weekend. This is a party after all," he said with a gleaming smile, and she glanced up at him.

Good God, he was irresistible when he smiled. It wasn't a natural occurrence. Rarely done. When he beamed, she felt as if the sun came bursting back, blazing into the sky after a frightening, thundering, dark storm.

"Y-yes."

Marcus? She was so used to thinking of him as Dr. Stewart, she had forgotten he had a first name. *Oh, sweet Jesus.* The sound of it seemed delightful to her ears, and her legs turned to jelly.

It was good to know he was holding her steady and close—if not, she could have swayed.

"Are you enjoying the party?" he went on in the same manner, his warm breath fanning her ear.

She answered in monosyllables. Erin was too nervous for any reasonable conversation, however short, unable to put a coherent sentence together. She shivered; a tremor took hold of her body.

***

"MISS BLAKE, are you okay? You are trembling." Marcus was holding her to his chest for the dance.

He could smell her sweet lavender, mixed with some other feminine perfume brand. He was used to her scent. It lingered in his office many times, well after she'd left. Sometimes, it drove him mad, and he had to open the

French doors to the garden to air the place. He would not have been able to focus otherwise.

Once or twice, when he had been too close to the edge, he'd cancelled her appointments, claiming a clash in his calendar schedule. The reality was he needed to avoid the woman. He could bet one of these days he was going to jump her bones, as the vernacular said, literally! He would if he was not careful. There were times he stayed away from her, avoiding her altogether.

So, her proximity on the dance floor and her scent were consuming him. He was used to controlling himself; if not, he would have given himself away long ago.

That evening, she mixed her scent with some other essence brand. To be honest, he didn't like it that way; he liked the simple lavender perfume that was so her.

His sister, Dr. Devlin, had mentioned once, she wanted to buy the lavender droplets that Miss Blake used in her bath. Since then, the thought of Miss Blake, naked, in her tub, infused in lavender, had given Marcus wet dreams! *For God's sake!* He'd been an adolescent the last time he had a wet dream!

So, he was suffering now, dancing with her without holding her tight to him, enveloping her within him, to feel her breasts grazing his chest. The more he thought of this, his cock had a life of his own with her so close to him.

"I'm tired, Doctor," she mumbled. "I am not used to parties anymore. I haven't been to one for over a year," she added, as they still moved in sync to the music.

He cleared his throat, trying to regain his full self-control before he spoke. "Then, I suggest you go to bed. You don't need to overdo it. I don't want you to tire yourself," he replied without hesitation, and exhaled. This took him out of jail, his semi hard-on ready to give him away.

"Bed?" she shrieked in a high-pitched voice.

"Yes, Miss Blake. I allowed you to attend the party, but it doesn't mean you have to stay up until the end. I don't want you ill in the morning. The night is at an end for you. We'll have another dance, and then I'll take you to your room," he said with finality. It was time to put some distance between them before something happened.

BED? Sleep? She was glad the loud music and the noise of the party had drowned her high-pitched voice when the doctor had given her marching orders.

The reason she was trembling… it was because of him, but she couldn't tell him that! She had lied and said she was tired. Erin cursed herself for being an idiot.

She felt his big palm on the small of her back, sending a thrill down below in her nether region, his other hand holding hers as they danced. It felt so good, so intimate. It had given her a slight tremor. For goodness' sake, she was not tired. She wished to be there, in his arms, dancing with him. All. Night. Long.

Sleep? Is he out of his mind? Who the hell can relax at the minute?

Erin had spent four months pining for Dr. Stewart, and now they were dancing. They were not cheek-to-cheek, but he was close enough. His breath fanned her ear when he spoke. Tight enough for her to smell his masculinity mingled with a citrus, fresh scent. Close enough for his gorgeousness to entice her, to make her head spin. She felt like licking his neck; he smelt so delicious, manly, and hot.

And he wants me to sleep? Jesus, the man is so oblivious to me! I mean nothing to him. Marcus is so out of my league. I am a patient, that's all I am to him. He's out of bounds to me for a reason. He doesn't care for me, no matter what Belinda or Lily say! Mine are only delusions; I have imagined things all these months. Yes, that's it, just my silly fantasies.

Her friends at the clinic were convinced Dr. Stewart fancied her, and they joked with her about it. They teased her incessantly. They were wrong, Erin was sure, and now she had the proof. He wanted to send her off to sleep. *Oh, the bear of a man!* Why would he dispatch her to bed if he cared for her because no! *He doesn't fancy me! That's why.*

Yes, she would like to hit the hay but with him atop her and his cock buried deep inside her. That kind of bed would be fine for her! But *sleep*! Erin cursed silently. She couldn't, even if she tried.

She looked up at him. His eyes found hers, and then they moved to her mouth. For a second, she stilled. She thought he was going to kiss her. *Wrong again!*

"Right!" he cracked on, his voice hoarse. "Time for bed, otherwise I won't allow you out again." And he yanked her by the hand and pulled her away from the dancing floor.

She missed her step, and he steadied her.

"Goodnight, Mollie, it was a lovely party. Miss Blake is tired, and she needs to rest," Marcus said to his hostess. Erin kissed Mollie on the cheek without a word and nodded to Zac, with a small smile on her lips.

Dr. Stewart grabbed her elbow and drew her away and into the house, up the stairs to her room.

"WHAT THE HELL is wrong with him?"

"What? Come, let's dance." Zac took his wife's hand, ignoring her statement, and they sauntered to the dance floor. He tugged her into his arms, in a close embrace, ready to move in tune to the music, but Mollie was miles away.

"Did you notice the look on Erin's face, I thought she was going to burst into tears! For heaven's sake, what's wrong with your friend?"

"What?"

"Marcus and Erin!"

"What about them?"

"Didn't you see her? I'll bet she would have easily stayed here, dancing with him."

"Well, she is his patient. He knows best; he is her doctor."

"Rubbish! Besides, he said so himself, Devlin is her doctor, not him!" Mollie's eyes narrowed with a deep frown on her face.

Zac pulled his head back to glance at his wife. He had a questioning look. "Umm…" He cocked his head to the side and stared at her.

"What? Why are you looking at me like that?"

"Mollie, let them be."

"Let them be? Are you mad? What am I going to do? Even if I wanted to, they are leaving on Monday morning. I probably won't see them for weeks unless I go to the clinic."

"Well, I am just saying. You have that face on you that precedes trouble. And I won't have it," he said, his sultry eyes warning her, a fiery expression in them.

She smiled sweetly at him. She placed her hands behind his neck, pulled him down to her until her lips touched his, kissing him deliciously. Zac forgot what he was saying.

THEY REACHED THE LANDING. They stopped outside Erin's bedroom.

"Sleep well," Marcus said. He didn't even know how it happened, or why. His body, having a will of its own, Marcus leaned over to give her a goodnight kiss on her cheek.

Not expecting it, she moved her head at that precise second, and the kiss ended up at one corner of her mouth, covering half of hers with his. He couldn't have landed the kiss on point if he tried. She flushed. Her bottom lip quivered, and she gasped, her eyes wide, staring at him. She mumbled a quick goodnight and went into her room swiftly. She shut the door in his face.

It was her opportunity to do something about it. She should have seized the moment, but she had chickened out! *You stupid, stupid woman!* she told herself. Her forehead rested against the door. Her heart was still thumping in her chest, so loud she thought it was going to burst out. She was as red as a beetroot. A small mercy that he couldn't see how that light kiss affected her.

Then she froze. She had not picked up his footsteps walking away. Was he still there? What was he doing?

Her breath halted altogether. She listened to the movement outside. *Is he waiting for me?* As she debated with herself, she heard his footsteps moving away. She wasn't sure if she felt relieved or disappointed. Oh, sweet Jesus, she was thirty-three, and she was behaving like a teenager with her first crush.

I suppose when you are in love… you are in love regardless of your age! What? In love? Was she in love with Marcus? Or was it lust? She'd had a two-year sex drought and was desperate for a good shag. Yes, that was it; not love, but lust. That was all.

I am just horny! she convinced herself.

God, the man could ignite her senses. If she didn't control herself, one of these days she was going to… *oh, bloody hell, take a cold shower!*

Or did she really want him? Oh, dear God, she was so confused. Perhaps it was for the best he had walked away.

She moved to the bed and plopped her backside on it. She lay there perfectly still, like a statue, her mind blank, for what seemed like an eternity. Then, she put her face in her hands and cried. She sat there and wept. She wasn't sure why she did it, but all the emotions of the past year came crashing down on her, hitting her soul with force, and they threatened to choke her. So, she sobbed.

Erin wept disconsolately for her dead twin brother and for missing her parents, God rest their souls. She shed tears for herself, for going off the rails and hurting people when she was at her worst. She cried her eyes out for being a wimp at everything, a useless human being.

Hope had abandoned her. Her emotions crushed her, and she felt dejected. Why she ever thought a man like Marcus would be interested in a hopeless woman like her? In a nutcase? It was a mystery to her, how she had even dared to contemplate such a possibility. No, he never would. And she wailed, all her insecurities assailing her at once. Erin couldn't say how long she cried until she heard a knock at the door.

She held her breath again, then she dried her tears with the ball of her hand. "Come in."

The door opened and Mollie came in, closing the door behind herself. "The light was on, and I thought I heard… never mind. I just wanted to check on you, Erin. Are you okay?" Her friend had a deep frown on her face.

"Yes, yes," she mumbled, struggling to look calm. She stood up and went to the mirror to peek at herself with an excuse, but when she saw her mascara running in black streaks across her face, she burst into tears again.

"Oh, darling." Mollie went to her with open arms, and the two girls hugged.

"That's okay. Let it out," her companion said, rubbing her back.

Mollie walked her to the bed and sat Erin there, caressing her hair. She picked up a hanky from the dressing table and handed it to her to dry her tears and nose. "What is it?" she asked, but Erin shrugged her shoulders. "Is it the doctor? Marcus?"

"Y-yes," Erin hiccupped while sobbing, and the floodgates opened again.

Mollie held her in her arms for a while. "What's he done?"

"N-nothing, that's the problem… He's done nothing!" Erin flashed red. She told her how she felt about the doctor.

Her companion gave way to a small laugh. "I see," Mollie said. She narrowed her eyes and was pensive for a while.

"You do?"

"Fine! Time to take action." She smiled, while Erin looked at her questioningly, not knowing what to expect.

"What do you mean?"

"Okay, here's what you'll do." Mollie explained her plan. Erin gawked at her open-mouthed, shaking her head.

Chapter 4

That night, memories came flooding back to him. His mind strayed to the very first time he saw her. *Oh, God!*

Marcus had met Erin long ago, way before she landed in his clinic. It was many years ago when her twin brother, Peter, with Finley, Zac, and Alex, plus four other young men with an experienced cox, had assembled an eight-rowing boat for the regatta. They were all experienced rowers, ready for the competitions on The River Thames. He had gone to watch his friends race. That was over fourteen years ago, a lifetime in his past.

Time faded into memories. This, a rather hazy one for him. Though, why was he experiencing now that same expanded feeling in his chest? Like that time, many moons in that distant past.

That day on the river, he recalled, he had seen her walk, talk and laugh in the company of others during the regatta. Above the vast expanse of the water, against the excitement and the crowds for the rowing races, he first set eyes on her, an angel.

All those years back, a delightful morning in early July, the sun was high and warm. He arrived at the usual marquee in Henley-on-Thames, on the left bank of the River Thames, like he did every year as part of the English social calendar. He intended to enjoy the day of rowing on the river. One day out of the five days of races at one of the most prestigious boat race events in the world, The Henley Regatta.

It was then he first saw Erin, a charming, tall young girl as she was then, with a light blue flowery dress, the same colour as the sky, a rosy, silky complexion, huge black eyes, and long dark hair. She was noble looking.

Erin had kindled something in his soul, in his heart. He would have vowed he had fallen in love with her on sight, but that seemed only a whim strengthened by his fantasies over the years.

That day on the river, he darted furtive glimpses at her during lunch at a vast table hosting a dozen guests. With so many people around, he could study her almost undisturbed.

Her twin brother introduced her to Marcus shortly after lunch. But like a restless butterfly, she soon fled on the bank of the river with her then-boyfriend. He caught another glimpse of her later that afternoon, smiling and exuberant. It stirred something in him.

His chest swelled with emotion watching her. She was resting on a blanket near the riverbank in the sun. A flurry of air blew a lock of her hair in and out of her face until she tucked it behind her ear. An image he would never forget. To this day, it was branded in his mind, so vivid as if it had been yesterday. Not that Erin had noticed him, anyway.

Even now, after four months at his clinic, she had not remembered meeting him, and Marcus had never mentioned it. Why would she recognise him after so long? If truth be told, she would not have remembered him the next day after the regatta, so besotted she was with her then-boyfriend.

After that, life had taken them in separate directions. Marcus married Penny over a year later. He loved his wife until her death two years ago; he had a happy life with her. He never regretted marrying her, and she had been all he wished for in a wife. After her death, he had thrown himself even more deeply into his work. But now he was alone again, lonely, and he missed the love of a woman.

He had never set eyes on Erin again, since that day at the regatta, until her arrival at his clinic four months ago. She was back in his life, at least in his professional life.

Though, through the years, he had not quite forgotten her. A latent, sweet vision that would resurface unannounced at the oddest of times, a fantasy of youth. From time to time, her laugh would ring in his ears like that day at the regatta. He clung to the memory, never getting over her. Like an unobtainable siren, with a hypnotic singing voice. Even to this day, he could remember her melodious laughter.

He shook his head to distance himself from those wild thoughts of bygone years. Back from his reverie, he tossed and turned in his bed. He was suffering the pains of hell!

An hour ago, Marcus had debated with himself outside Erin's bedroom if he should follow her in. He hesitated for a few moments. He almost gave in, muttering under his breath. The temptation had been too great. But something held him back. He couldn't compromise his professional relationship with her, his career, his clinic. Many people depended upon him. So, Marcus had marched on to his room instead.

The way she took fright when his kiss half-landed on her lips had scared her witless. He could tell. He had seen it on her face, in her big, black eyes, wide open, questioning him. She practically ran away from him and hid in her room. He decided not to push her, not to rush her, and for his sins, he retreated.

Marcus was in bed. He had enjoyed Mollie's party, but now he could not sleep. Oh, hell, no! He was wide awake. Restless… lying on his side, then a second later, flat on his back. Then, he turned on his other side, next, he stretched on his stomach, and back and forth as if he had a twitch and a bed full of spiders.

A million thoughts flashed through his mind. His reflections were on the lady, two doors down the hallway. The kiss had half-scorched his lips and almost given her a coronary.

He'd been right on one thing. Her lips were soft and plump. They felt delicious under his, even in that microsecond he had tasted them. Marcus would have liked nothing better than to do it again. He wished now he had taken the plunge and damn the consequences. *The hell with everything!* His professional life be damned! And if he didn't do it soon, he would go insane with desire for Erin. He would lose his mind.

He remembered his sister's words before he started for the party earlier that evening. "Enjoy Mollie's party, Marcus. Please, please, make sure you do!" His younger sister, Dr. Julia Devlin, pleaded with him before he left, "I really hope you will. And when you come back to the clinic on Monday, you'd better be yourself again."

"Myself again? I don't know what you mean," he echoed, puzzled, with a crease between his brows.

"You are behaving like a bear, Marcus. I realise you have a tremendous amount of work to do, the clinic on your shoulders, and so much more on your mind. But you'd better calm down and relax. Find yourself a girl tonight, if I may say so, before you drive us all bloody crazy! And you know which lady I mean, too. Don't forget; I am her doctor, not you. I declare, both of you need a good dose of that therapy if you get my meaning. She'll feel a hundred times stronger, too, I assure you. You'll do a lot more for her in one night than my analysis would do in weeks. I can bet my career on that! Besides, she's quite well now, almost ready for the world again. She's just nervous, that's all. And I dare say, the woman would like a bit of you, too! But above all, my dear brother, I must deal with you, as you are getting on my nerves in your present state. So, take my advice," Dr. Devlin said half in jest and half seriously, scowling at him, and he could not blame her, either.

Marcus glared at her in astonishment, but he had to admit she was right. He had been insufferable with his sister, with his staff, and with his patients, for weeks. Though he had scoffed at Julia and feigned offence at her words, he could not deny it. His level-headed sister had a point. His calm, his powerful yet quiet charm, his composed personality were nowhere to be seen in recent months. It disturbed even him.

From the minute Erin landed back in his life, he had withstood months of torturing himself about her. But he came to the realisation, too, admitting it to himself, *Dear Good, I worship the woman!*

It amused him it had taken his little sister's words to realise the reason for his malaise. The one that was millennia old, and it had forever afflicted humans, the one of the heart.

Love! I am in love with Erin Blake, bloody hell! he repeated to himself. He rolled his eyes, thinking about it, and his mouth gave out a great puff of air. He snorted at the notion, despite his grim humour.

It was one of those hot and clammy August nights, which didn't help to beckon sleep, either. He yanked the coverlet from his body. Marcus was flustered, disconcerted at his emotions. He finally grasped his sentiments for the woman. It caused him to break into a sweat, and the hot night had nothing to do with it. He got up from bed and put the lights on. He needed a drink of water, and he gulped the entire glass in one go. He could have done with something stronger than water, given the self-revelation, and tonight, he had been so close to giving way to his passion for her.

He opened the window to take some fresh air. The summer breeze cooled him somehow. He mumbled a curse, and to that one, more black curses followed out of his mouth until the knock at the door thwarted his foul language with his realisation.

Marcus took a deep breath; he was only wearing his boxers, so he put on his dressing gown.

He looked at the time; it was two am.

"Come in," he said, sitting on the windowsill.

"Mollie!" It perplexed him to see the girl come in. "Is everything okay?"

"I am sorry to disturb you, Marcus, but it's Erin…"

"Erin?" He stood up abruptly and walked up to her. "Is she all right?"

"Oh, yes, yes. She is fine. But she is partying hard, and she is a bit overexcited. I thought you may want to know, ahem… before she does something stupid," Mollie replied, and she shifted on her feet.

"The party? But I left her in her room!"

"You might have done so, Marcus. But she is back at the party right now, taking full advantage of it. Don't get me wrong, I want my guests to enjoy themselves. Perhaps she is a little exuberant now you are not around." Mollie's baby blues were wide and innocent, expectant. She waved her hand in the air to emphasise her point.

"Exuberant?" he cried out with incredulity and narrowed his eyes on her.

"Aha!"

He cocked his head and watched her for a moment, then he mumbled a curse under his breath. "I'll be down in a minute as soon as I have dressed. Keep an eye on her until I get there."

"HE'S COMING, darling, so you'd better get on the dance floor and shake your booty. Do your dance; come on. This is George, a friend, he's doing his masters at Uni. He knows the plan. I've promised him dinner at my house for the next two weeks to do this. He'll do anything for my cook's food. He'll help you with the sexy dance moves. George, this is Erin."

"My pleasure! I've heard a lot about you from Mollie and Kathryn these few months. I feel as if I know you. Sexy dancing moves, yes! I'm all for it. I'll teach you the moves," he ventured with a wide grin.

"What sexy moves?" Erin shrieked in a high pitch tone when it dawned on her what the plan really entailed, darting her wide eyes from George to her companion in mild panic. She smoothed the alluring dress Mollie had just given her. Since Erin was a few inches taller than her friend, though it fit her well, it was quite short on her.

Erin's long legs looked breathtaking under that dress and in high heels. This red frock was hot compared to the more sedate evening gown she'd worn earlier. This sizzling little number hugged her figure divinely. It had a vertiginous plunging neckline. She had borrowed the dress from her friend, but her breasts, being larger than Mollie's, spilled abundantly out of it. Erin formed a seductive image, a temptress-like vision of herself. Her hands smoothed the dress as if she craved to lengthen it. She kept on patting her breasts anxiously, too, as if she wanted to will her tits to grow smaller and back inside the dress, as if to say *boobs, please hide!* She was too self-conscious to feel at ease, it was unreal!

"Oh, for God's sake, Erin, stop fidgeting with the damn dress! You look awesome. Doesn't she, George?" Mollie blurted, shaking her head in disapproval at her companion's nervousness.

"Ravishing!" he said, lifting his eyebrows in quick succession, reinforcing the point with a wide smile.

Erin blushed, not used to compliments.

"Didn't I show you how Imelda and George were dancing earlier, hey? That's what you've got to do," Mollie whispered in her ear.

"But I can't..." Erin squealed as she flushed again in a deeper shade of red. Her mouth went dry, and her tongue stuck to her palate.

Her companion narrowed her eyes on her and shook her head.

Sweet Jesus, I am so out of my depth here! This was not in Erin's shy nature. She wished she had not agreed to this silliness, but Dr. Stewart annoyed her by ordering her to the room when there was a party in full swing. In particular when they had been dancing together, and the brute had ceased all her fun. Not to mention, Mollie made her plan sound so easy...

Flipping heck! Now she was not so sure.

Erin took a deep breath. She couldn't fault the handsome young man, or his sexy movements, she had to admit. But Erin wasn't a good dancer. She wasn't even used to this if truth be told. She felt awkward enough dancing with Dr. Stewart, let alone having seductive dance moves with George, as her companion was willing her to do.

"I am going to look ridiculous," she said through gritted teeth, and her lips pressed in a thin line.

"Darling," Mollie said patiently, as if talking to an unresponsive child, "Marcus is on his way down. You've got a minute, at most two, before he gets here. You must make your mind up. Do you want to do this? If so, bloody dance! If not, no harm done. You return to your bedroom and when he is here, I will tell him it was a false alarm, and you went back to bed. Up to you!"

Erin glanced at them in turn. George had the widest smile and a twinkle of mischief in his eyes, and when a waiter passed with a tray, she grabbed two flutes of champagne. She downed them, one after the other, in huge gulps, knowing full well she promised Dr. Devlin "no drinking." Dr. Stewart had himself reinforced this point, only allowing her to come to the party with the strictest proviso she would drink no alcohol. Only soft drinks allowed, as she was still on medication.

But desperate times called for desperate measures. Besides, she was almost herself again. She needed a bit of audacity to do what Mollie suggested. A boldness she didn't feel right now, a daring she didn't have, but she went for it. She couldn't backtrack.

"Right! George? Dance it is, then. Mind you, I am rubbish at this." She put down the empty glasses on a tray from a passing waiter. She grabbed another drink in the midst, too. She downed half of the third flute of champagne; she needed Dutch courage for this.

Oh, Good God!

"I'll signal when he is here. You are not supposed to drink. I want to help you but drinking——" Mollie chastised.

"Shush, Mollie! Too late for that!" she mumbled to her friend. "George?" Erin glanced at the young man for instructions, still holding the glass of champagne.

"Just follow what I do, and you'll be fine. Hey, your boyfriend isn't violent, is he?" He put his hand on the small of her back and propelled her through the crowd of dancers onto the centre of the platform.

Her breath hitched. "He is not my boyfriend!"

Marcus reached the marquee and looked around.

Mollie waved at her, showing that Dr. Stewart had arrived.

"He's here, George!" Erin trembled, her eyes wide, petrified. She felt rooted to the spot, unable to move. Dazed, she took small breaths.

"Hey, hey. Relax! Take it easy, it's just dancing," George said in a calm voice. He caressed her cheek, seeing the woman so put out. "Now, close your eyes. It's better that way, and listen to the music, nothing else. Clear your mind. Focus on the sound. Can you do that? Hear the trumpets. The drums. The rhythms," he murmured reassuringly, calmly, in a soothing silvery tone, with a perfect posture, his shoulders rolled back, ready and full of confidence.

"Y-yes," she stammered, biting her bottom lip, and she fidgeted with her dress again. She inhaled and nodded with a small smile.

He transmitted confidence to her with his self-assurance. "Good, stop fidgeting with your dress. You are a beautiful woman, Erin. Tall, so very tall, stunning! I'll hold you, there is nothing to worry about. Put your arms around my collar. Careful with that glass of champagne, though," he went on.

As Erin did so, George circled her waist with his arm and pulled her to him. Her body plastered to his, and she gasped. "Ooh..." she muttered and opened her eyes wide.

"Nothing to fear. Close your eyes, I said. Now, sway, Erin. Just follow the movement of my body with yours. Listen to the music, focus on the sound and my body," he whispered in her ear.

She was shaking. Embarrassed, she was so close to the young man, but she closed her eyes again. The moment she did so and inhaled, she relaxed in George's arms. As she then listened to the music, she followed his body's moves with hers as he twirled and swayed with her in his arms.

As Erin focused on the rhythms, on his scent and his body tight to hers with its undulating movements, as if by magic, she found herself dancing sexily with the young man, despite herself.

Not the most graceful dancer in the world, granted! But they rocked to the beat. Their bodies were as close to each other as Monday and Tuesday.

"WHERE IS SHE?" Dr. Stewart grimaced at the edge of the platform.

"She is dancing, there!" Mollie pointed in her friend's direction, while all she heard from him was an unrepeatable expletive as his eyes landed on Erin.

Mollie spun to him with an amused expression. Her plan was working.

"My apologies," he took a deep breath, "I don't swear in front of a lady, b-but..." he ventured, not knowing what to say, "She shouldn't be drinking, the medication..." Marcus mumbled, trying to recover from the shock of seeing Erin dancing like a siren, with a handsome young fellow, in a skimpy hot, short, red dress.

"That's why I called you. I know. She's had several drinks," she said, milking the situation and raising a sculpted brow.

He looked at Erin as she danced. *Her eyes are closed, for God's sake, the bloody minx!*

"Who the hell is that man?" he grunted, despite himself.

"Oh, he is just a friend; his name is George. He is harmless. That's how young people dance these days, you know. He loves the girl over there, you see." Mollie pointed to Imelda, in a corner, watching the dancers with a frown on her face.

"He's dancing with the wrong woman then," he murmured, more to himself.

"So is Erin!" she whispered, staring at Marcus, and his eyes grew wide at her.

"Ahem…" He tried to clear his throat to say something, but nothing came out.

"Well, I suggest, you get her!"

"Oh, what the hell…" And he marched off towards the dancers.

———

"DO you mind if I have a word with Erin? It's important," he said to the young fellow.

"Oh, Marcus! It's okay, George. He's my doctor." Erin spoke with her eyes wide, apprehension raising her heartbeat. Her voice sounding pitchier than usual.

"I am not your doctor. Dr. Devlin is, and you promised her no alcohol. I ratified her consent and allowed you here under those strict orders. You are breaking my rules," Dr. Stewart blurted with a stern expression on his face.

"Umm… uh," George mumbled, "I'll leave you to it."

Her dancing partner swiftly retreated, while Marcus yanked the flute of champagne out of her hands, neither of them noticing the young man had gone.

"How dare you! It's just one drink," she said, scowling at him.

"With the waft of alcohol coming from you, Miss Blake, I say, you are lying to me. I don't tolerate lies or patients breaking my rules. You know that," Dr. Stewart dictated as he raked a hand through his hair and his eyes narrowed on her.

He was preaching to her. She rolled her eyes and hissed like a cat. She'd had enough of his domineering attitude. "Bugger off, Marcus!" Erin spat. *The pompous ass, who the hell does he think he is?* And she turned her back on him. She blanked him and waved at George instead.

Marcus's jaw dropped. He blinked, suddenly realising she had just told him to bugger off. Incredible! The foolish woman! A shadow flashed across his face, and his countenance darkened, as if a stream of murky clouds were enveloping a blue sky, ready for a thunderstorm. "Right, that's it! You crossed the line, sweetheart!" And he circled her upper arm tightly with his big hand, holding her tight as he finished, in one gulp, the glass of champagne he had taken from her.

She yelped at the sudden tug of her arm. *Sweetheart?* Then he dragged her off the dance floor. She almost lost her balance twice as he hauled her out of the marquee. She held on to him with her other hand to stay upright. "What the hell are you doing! Let me go; I am dancing."

"Not anymore, you ain't!" he muttered under his breath as he took long strides, shaking his head, staring right ahead.

"What? Stop right now."

"Let's see... First, you don't tell me to bugger off, hiss or roll your eyes at me; two, you've broken the promise to my sister of no drinking; third, you have broken my rules when I allowed you here under those same strict orders of no alcohol. Fourth—" he pointed out as he dragged her along.

"There is more? Flipping heck!" she said facetiously and scoffed.

"Oh, there is, my dear Miss Blake. Believe you me!"

"What the fuck! Quit calling me Miss Blake if you are going to manhandle me. Fuck, stop!" The booze was making her bold and dirty mouthed, as he pulled her through the garden and into the house.

He paused at her foul language and swung to her, his eyes piercing hers. "If you say *fuck* at me one more time, Miss Bla... Erin, your ass will be on fire right here! Do I make myself clear?"

"This is silly. I was just enjoying myself." But he grabbed her wrist and marched on his way, pulling her with him. "Stop, I said. Do you hear me?" she went on, trying to free herself.

"You need a lesson in respect, poppet. Next time you wish to break my rules, or swear at me, you'll remember this night!"

Did he just call me 'poppet'? She laughed, though it was a nervous laugh. She wasn't sure how to take his sudden surge of familiarity and that command of his, combined.

He darted a look at her full of fire; it made her gulp. But he would not intimidate her, not tonight!

"Don't be ridiculous. And slow down. I can't keep up with you!" she blabbered as he was dragging her unceremoniously through the house. They were climbing the sweeping staircase.

"With those long, bare legs under that very short dress? Hard to believe!"

"What?"

"Which reminds me, fourth rule. And I mean it! Never, ever, wear such a tempting tiny dress again! Do you hear me? I can see your panties."

"Liar! You can't."

"Oh, yea, sure I can! A sudden move with that short dress of yours, and I will."

"No! You won't. I am not wearing any panties. You'll see my ass." She had a fit of giggles and raised her hand over her mouth to silence her laugh. She couldn't help herself. God, that was the alcohol talking. She was provoking him now!

He froze on the spot as they approached the upstairs landing. He remained still for a second, then turned slowly to her. Marcus computed her words, then scanned her from head to toe in a slow motion.

Being on the receiving end of his scowl, she lifted her chin in rebellion with a glower on her face. But he stared her down.

She blushed to a deep red at the fierce flash of his eyes. Erin was sure she had seen desire there, mingled with other sentiments she couldn't read, but he said nothing.

His eyes settled on her breasts, spilling over the dress, and instinctively she placed a hand over them.

"Too late to cover them, don't you think?" He scorned her, deriding her gesture, mimicking it. "When half the bloody nation has seen your pair in all their glory," he ended with sarcasm.

She gasped at his arrogance and narrowed her eyes at him. But before she could have time to reply, he yanked her by the wrist, moving her along with him. He paced down the hallway, tugging her along.

"Stop! Where the hell are you taking me, let me go. This minute! Do you understand? Or I'll scream!"

He halted. He dropped the hold on her, spun and flashed at her again. His eyes were thundering on her, the fire in them scorching her. He was becoming more incensed by the minute, and she could feel the billowing of his rampant, bad temper in the air. It made her nervous; she was in an uncharted territory with him like this. All she had known for four months was the calm and composed doctor, a rather dictatorial one, but nevertheless composed and controlled. She wasn't sure what to make of this Marcus. But if truth be told, she was rather excited at the prospect of finding out more of this side of him. She gulped.

Suddenly, he advanced on her. But in her haste to shrink from him, she moved sideways instead, and she trapped herself against the hallway wall. Their eyes locked for a second. She didn't move a muscle, spellbound, her bosom heaving with trepidation. He leaned on her, and his body closed on hers. She gave out a shriek of surprise as he did so, at his proximity.

Erin was a tall woman. Marcus was still a few inches taller. At that precise moment, he seemed to tower over her, huge as he was. Massive and threatening, and oh, so damn dashing, she almost wet herself. Her pulse thundered in her ears with apprehension. But her pussy was soaked. Somehow this handsome man seemed lustful and full of promise, scary, too. Oh, by God, how she craved him!

She wanted to shrink and to dare him on, taunting him and dreading the situation. Perspiration erupted on her upper lip at his closeness. Even though she had dreamt of this moment for months, now that it was upon her, she relished it and she dreaded it.

He placed his palms flat to his elbows on the wall, either side of her, thus she couldn't move away from him. He trapped her in!

Her breath hitched, and she looked up at him again. She could smell his scent, so fresh and masculine, his warm breath fanning her face.

"Scream, are you?" he whispered, and then his lips landed on hers, forcefully, full of yearning and passion.

After the first second or two of astonishment, the thrill of the kiss set into her bones, deep. It fired her up! As if he'd turned on a switch, the heat inside her burst open, spreading and rolling in lustful waves to every cell of her body. She closed her eyes and opened for him with want and desire.

His tongue was inside her mouth, tasting her, having his fill of her, sparring with hers. Their mouths danced to a tune of craving and wonderment at each other.

He grabbed her arms and crossed them above her head, holding them there, as his body pressed to hers, harder. She felt faint and wonderful, aching for him. She wanted this moment never to end.

Another small shriek escaped her. But it was soon muffled by his lips again. He kissed her with force, lust, and love. As if an ardent and blazing fever had taken command of his senses, with all the mingled sentiments a man could feel for a woman. He owned her mouth, ravishing her, transmitting his passion to her.

The kiss stirred her blood, her limbs turned to jelly. A good job he had a hard grip on her arms crossed above her head; he kept her from falling in a heap of molten heat on the floor. Her body's temperature was scorching her, as if fused into the hotness of the Earth's molten core. She radiated heat.

"Yes, I dare say you'll scream when I am finished with you," he whispered when the kiss ended, his silvery bass tone rasp and harsh now, "but you'll beg me to do it all over again."

He didn't allow her to respond. He claimed her mouth, utterly kissing her with an uncontrollable burning, as their tongues tangoed in a delirium of passion.

She was almost limp. It dazzled her. Her head twirled in a whirlwind of need and want. The ache at the apex of her thighs demanded release. Her pussy throbbed.

He pulled his head back and looked at her. Her eyes were closed, her breathing laboured. A wide smile formed on his lips, seeing her totally under his control. Then Marcus released her arms, as they came down limp at her side. He circled her upper arm and yanked her with him towards his bedroom.

She gasped at the sudden movement. "What are you doing? Stop!" she whimpered, still in a daze. In reality, she did not want this to end any time soon.

"Oh, don't think for a moment because I kissed you, I have forgotten your disrespect, your misbehaviour! You cannot drink and take medication; that's a no-no! You know it, and I warned you!"

"Stop being silly Marcus."

"Silly?" He gave her another dark look. He wrapped his hand around her gorgeous ass, having a good fill of it. Then, he pinched it, and smacked her backside hard as they arrived at his bedroom door.

She yelped, not expecting this. "Aw, aw, are you insane? Let me go."

"You'll go when I tell you to go." He smiled at her, and a wide grin opened, having enjoyed smacking her bottom.

Chapter 5

His overbearing manner, that of a rule-mongering, domineering man, stirred her. *Dr. Stewart is happy only when he's giving orders, the damn sod,* Erin thought in indignation. *Who the hell does he think he is to strut me like this! At his will!*

Oh, but she couldn't get enough of his kisses. No, she wanted more! She was confused.

At first, he had dismissed her. He had sent her to bed, for goodness' sake! As if she were a child. Commanding her! Then taking charge. Now kissing her! His kisses were melting her body with his heat and passion, and she wished for more, but still… he was too much to take.

Though he was what she wanted, and she wouldn't want him any other way. He agitated her and aroused her.

She felt insecure and apprehensive about the outcome of where this was leading her. She was in a confused arousal, not understanding exactly where she stood with him or his intentions.

He was intense, but a gorgeous beast of a man! Sweet Jesus, that smile, though; it was adorable! Brief as it was. As he smiled at her, a warmth surged through her body, igniting her.

He had reduced her to a wanton, lascivious, needy woman with a gleaming, out of control, feverish pussy, in urgent need of his cock. She felt hot, and the August heat wasn't even close to the scorching smouldering of her body now, her throbbing tight depths a testament to that.

Four months of yearning and burning for him had vented all at once in her, exploding without warning, like a ticking bomb. She would not survive this night! *God help her!*

She could not deny the lustful and salacious thoughts the doctor aroused in her. The longing she thwarted every time she was in his office. She had a wet dream about him early one morning, at thirty-three!

Now, she was waiting in anticipation, for the taking, for the plucking! As if she was coming out of the oven. Ready to be eaten alive by those passionate kisses of his. She would be ecstatic if he gobbled her up!

The pinch on her bottom and the hard smack he gave her, as much as she felt the sting, Erin had liked it a lot. A sharp pang of yearning had gone straight to her clit, making it throb when he smacked her. And with those delirious kisses beforehand, he sent her spiralling into the stratosphere, floating in the universe of lust and desire, not wanting to come back to Earth.

Lord, am I up for this? she worried.

Other than discussions on her treatment, they had hardly spoken of little else.

She was sweltering. The heaviness between her legs spoke volumes. Her body was telling her exactly what she needed and with whom. At that precise moment, the whom… was the man right there, kissing her lips salaciously. She wanted Marcus more than anything in the world. For goodness' sake, the thought drenched her. If he touched her again, she would dribble like a broken tap. Butterflies were causing havoc in her tummy at his imperious manner and what more he could do to her.

She gulped, looking at him. Dare she say she loved him? She hadn't felt so entranced with any man. Lustful thoughts crashed in her mind and soul, just breathing his scent.

He annoyed the hell out of her with his rules-mongering dictatorship. Though, if she had to be honest with herself, his dictatorial manners raised her pulse. Deep inside her, a part of her adored this autocratic man and his imperious, absolute manners.

She didn't know she craved this, a commanding man. Something visceral stirred in her when he did this. Something she wanted and had never had. It twisted her insides into a mush, wanting to say, "yes, sir" to him after every command, every order he gave her.

All these different emotions clashed and rioted inside her from this one man in a bat of an eyelash. It bewildered her. It confused her. Oh, sweet Jesus, Erin desired him so badly, she didn't care anymore. Whatever it was, she would take it, without question.

Marcus dragged her into his bedroom with him. He closed the door and released her as he locked it.

She shivered. She moved to the middle of the room, panting, not knowing what to do. Or what to expect, and if she had to admit, also a little scared. She stood there perfectly still, watching him. Her apprehension rose even more. She had wished this for God knows how long… but now that it was upon her, she felt nervous. The fact she had not made love for ages worried her. Would he like her after all?

"What's the matter, the cat got your tongue? So silent suddenly?" he said, seeing her wringing her hands and white as a sheet, "You aren't frightened of me, are you?"

"Yes, I mean, no. I don't know," she mumbled and smoothed her dress with her palms several times.

"Is it yes, or no?"

"Uh… hem," she cleared her throat. "Maybe just a little," she whispered, and he raised an elegant brow to her as she continued to smooth her frock.

"Stop fidgeting! Though it is a very short, silly, scant dress, you look beautiful in it."

"T-thank you. I think it's a compliment, isn't it?" she asked, unsure.

He smiled and nodded. "Those high heels, so tall… there is so much of you, and I want to see it all, Erin. Come here," he commanded.

"Why?"

"Oh, for God's sake, woman! Do you have to question everything I say? Come here, I said."

And she whisked herself into motion and came close to him. He caressed her face with his knuckles, and she leaned into them, stroking them with her cheek.

He held a lock of her hair in his hand and let it loose, slithering it through his fingers. Marcus took another, brought it to his nose and inhaled. "God, your scent drives me crazy! I had wafts of lavender in my office for weeks." And he put his arms around her waist and crushed her to him. She gave out a small shriek of surprise, but his lips dropped on hers with the force of a hurricane, tasting her, savouring the depths of her mouth, utterly kissing her, curving her backwards with his powerful kiss.

She was breathless.

His head went back, and his eyes locked with hers, searching, wondering, and he smiled. A wide grin spread from ear to ear with the simple pleasure of holding her into his arms.

She took a deep breath and smiled back.

He leaned forward again, and this time he took her mouth, slowly, gently. His hands went to her face, holding her tenderly in place. He brushed his lips on hers, lightly, seductively. Then he kissed her more deeply, not too hard, not too soft, exploring her mouth with reverence. Trying to acquaint himself with hers, rather than taking over. Gently giving her space, too, her turn to explore his mouth, to get to know him. And they kissed sweetly for a while, caressing each other. His hands roamed softly on her body. He then kissed the hollow of her neck, a small titillating lick of his tongue followed.

A moan escaped her.

He nibbled at her earlobe, teasing her, repeatedly, and then back to her mouth.

A little dribble spilled over from her pussy, and she moaned again in his mouth. He grunted a guttural sound at hearing her moan of pleasure, at the delight he was bestowing on her. He ended the kiss and looked at her.

His thumb went to her lips and he caressed them, while she kissed his thumb with tiny little kisses, holding his hands.

"Oh, my love, I've been wanting to do this for months," he whispered.

She smiled coyly, nodding, and replied, "Me, too."

"First things first, sweetheart," he emphasised, leaving her side and walking off. He took his jacket off, rolled his shirt sleeves up, and sat on the couch at the bottom of his bed.

"Hm?" she mumbled, "what are you doing?"

"Lift your dress to your waist, darling, and come here," he said, in full control, his usual unflappable temperament seeming to have materialised as if by magic. He was enjoying this.

"What?" she said as her eyes went almost out of orbit.

"You heard me, darling, now like a good girl, here, on my lap! You don't think I have forgotten your disrespect, do you?"

"What the hell, M-Marcus?" she stammered.

"Aha! See my point, as much as I am eager to make love to you, poppet, you need to learn a lesson. No disrespecting me or disregarding my rules! The reason I allowed you to come to the party was under the strictest rule of No Drinking! Understood?"

"I only had one drink," she murmured.

"One? I take it from an excellent source you had several drinks, so don't lie to me. And when I said no alcohol, I meant it. None. But that's not all. You told me to bugger off, used awful language. And now you are lying. That won't do! Is that clear?"

"M-Marcus, I-I..." she tried, but no words came out.

"I won't allow you to make a mockery of things, when I give you an order and it's for your own good, always, remember that. Make no mistake, you follow it. Understood, and no disrespect as you go about it, either. Come here."

"You are not serious!"

"Now, sweetheart, why would I stop kissing that beautiful mouth of yours, if there wasn't a good reason for it? Ah? Here, now! Don't make me say it again. Haven't you been spanked before?"

"Spanked? No, of course not! Don't be silly." She laughed, and he raised a fine brow to her and beckoned her with his index finger.

"Well, if someone had, perhaps you wouldn't be so disobedient and disrespectful. Here, please. I don't want to drag you again. When I say come here, you do it. Here! *Now*!" he said, his last word a peremptory command.

She jolted into motion and stood by his side in a flash.

He grabbed her wrist and pulled her face down onto his lap.

She shrieked. "What the hell. No!" she cried out, but he landed a first set of smacks over her backside unexpectedly over her dress, and she let out a scream. It took her breath away.

"Shush, or they'll hear you above the music in the garden."

"Marcus..." She struggled to get up, but his arm was firm around her waist, and he clasped her arm in his hand, tightening her to him.

He pulled her frock up to her waistline, and it flabbergasted him. "Bloody hell, it's true! No panties, girl," he said, admiring her silky, creamy, round buttocks. He whistled a low, long drawn-out whistle. "Beautiful arse, my love, but if you go out with no panties again, without my permission, you'll be in deep trouble. I'll tell you when to and when not to wear them. Understood?" He smacked her with a thundering whack, his palm imprinted on her velvety skin in no time at all.

"Aw, aw, I told you I—" But a hard smack halted her speech and then another until speaking was impossible.

Whack! Whack! Whack!

She shrieked in agony. Her butt soon felt as if it was blistering. The August warmth, nothing compared to the fiery heat on her behind.

"You are undisciplined, unruly. This will be a reminder to you in case you want to misbehave. I demand absolute obedience. It's for your own good, darling. No disrespect, either, do you hear me?"

"Please, Marcus..." she pleaded. Her ass was glowing red like a fire engine in the midday sun. It stung, and it burned, and her raucous complaints were of no consequence as he went about his business of delivering powerful smacks on the crest of her glorious globes.

Tears flowed on her face. The sting as he toasted her derrière with his hand made her breathless. She wasn't able even to think. Erin became silent, limp, and took the spanking, whimpering under her breath. She felt humiliated he could see her bare ass like this, not to mention her other bits.

The bewildering thing was the more he smacked her back end, the more her insides flipped in anticipation. It flared the heat at her core, already at boiling point with his kisses, and now, with this, turning her into a hot mess of want, passion and craving. She had not imagined her reaction to spanking.

Her damp pussy throbbed. She wished he would take her there and then. She wanted to make frantic love to him. Despite her burning plump arse, in a sort of weird way, she was enjoying it. It ignited her desire all the more. She felt embarrassed at these contrasting emotions, pain and lust.

Another bunch of wallops from his hands bounced on her buttocks. The unbearable sting fuelled her hunger for him. She could not save a deep, throaty, lustful moan.

He halted. Marcus placed his warm hand on her scorching scarlet flesh for a few moments. He caressed her ass, patting it gently. "Are you okay?" He peered down at her, and she just nodded without a word, sniffing, but she couldn't help another whine as he rubbed her.

"Ahh…" She struggled to disguise her heavy arousal.

"Do you want me, my love?" he asked her tenderly, still caressing her backside. A big smile formed on his lips at seeing her like this, his cock having stirred throughout the spanking, wanting to take part in the action, too.

"N-no," she lied to him. She was mortified, but she would not admit she was dying to have him between her thighs. She shook her head, her cheeks burning.

"Hmm, let's see." He slid his fingers from the crack of her butt to her drenching slit, teasingly. "Now… what did I say about no lies?" And four consecutive whacks cracked on her derrière.

"M-Marcus, please." It only made her want him more.

"Then, tell me the truth, do you want me to fuck you?"

"Y-yes."

"Are you sure?"

"Oh, God! Yes, please do it."

"What, my love? What do you want me to do?" he asked, still rubbing her butt.

She moaned in arousal. "Oh, yes! Fuck me. Do it. For heaven's sake, please, take me!" she blurted out.

"Good! Because you are soaked, darling, and that's exactly what I want to do. This pussy now belongs to me." His fingers moved to the length of her slit, teasing her with his fingertips. He brought his index to his mouth and licked it. "Jesus, Erin, you taste amazing."

Then it slid inside her again. She shrieked in pure ecstasy at his touch. But he soon released her, and she moaned, disappointed.

"Greedy, are you, poppet?" He pulled her up to him and sat her on his lap. He cleared her long, dark hair from her face tenderly and wiped a few tears lingering on the corners of her eyes. He kissed her forehead and stole a small kiss on her lips. "So, do we understand each other now?" he asked her, still caressing her.

"Yes. I am sorry." She nodded, and he smiled.

He lifted her chin and as he looked at her, he brushed his lips on her cheeks softly. He took her mouth in a deep kiss as he slid his digits into her sweet, soaked centre. She gasped, not expecting it.

"Gorgeous, my girl. You are," he murmured as he pleasured her. Her eyes lowered. He raised her face to him with his other hand. "Keep your eyes on me, darling, I want to see you when you come." And he thrust in her while she panted low, whimpering sounds as his fingers increased in speed and depth inside her pussy. He retreated again.

"Oh," she said, mourning his touch, needing release. He scooped her up into his arms and moved towards the bed. He placed her down on it. Marcus unzipped her dress and pulled it over her head.

"Jesus, Erin, no bra, either. You were wearing nothing under this silly, little frock? Dancing with that young chap! Incredible." And he grabbed both of her ankles with one big hand and raised her legs up straight in the air, while he stood at the foot of the bed. He blistered her scarlet bottom several times, harshly, until it burned. It was during this second spanking, with all the pleasure his fingers had already bestowed on her pussy, that her insides gave way, and with a mix of purrs, moans, and whimpers, she climaxed hard.

"M-Marcus," she muttered, thrashing about, the sensations taking hold of her frame as her release burst into rolling waves of ecstasy. This was something new and thrilling for Erin. Her orgasm hit her long and protracted with her legs still up in the air while he smacked her ass.

He stopped smacking her, releasing her. He regarded her for a moment. A proud smile formed on his lips, and he leaned on her for a soft kiss. "I wonder, darling, if after this, you will be more inclined to misbehave. So, you can come while I smack you! Did you like that?" Then he ravished her mouth.

She nodded. Erin had felt nothing like this before, intense, so powerful. She was embarrassed the roasting of his firm hand on her plump flesh had driven a mighty orgasm out of her.

He trailed his hand over her naked body. He pinched her tits, rubbed them, and then sucked each nipple. He stood and walked away from the bed. He glanced at her, totally spent on the bed, while he took his clothes off. He stripped down until he reached his boxers, and when he discarded them, his massive cock popped out to greet her, bright and ready to fence.

A little tremor shook her frame at his beauty. Wide shoulders tapered into a trim waist, and in between, a wall of hard, sculpted chest muscles. Powerful thighs that went down on very long legs held his tall and majestic body. All this splendour was now hers. She couldn't believe it, and she couldn't wait for that massive cock to shake her as his spanking had.

HE HAD WAITED months to do this. Once or twice, he came close to losing it. Now that she was in front of him, for the taking, he was not in a hurry. He wanted to enjoy her, slowly and plenty.

"Open your legs, darling," he whispered as he captured her lips, and her eyes went big at him in surprise.

He stood by the edge of the bed to watch her.

"Please, love," he encouraged her.

"Marcus, I-I…"

Though she was no virginal maiden, she felt ashamed to open like this, at point blank, for him to have a sinfully good look.

"It's okay, darling, there is no shame in this." He smiled, sensing her embarrassment. She blushed scarlet but complied. She opened her legs a little, but he leaned over and placed his hands on her thighs, pressing them down, opening them.

She made a whimpering sound. "Oh, I—"

"It's fine, Erin, you are beautiful. You shouldn't be ashamed to show me how lovely you are. Inside and out."

As he dragged her bottom to the edge of the bed, she whimpered at her sore butt. Then, he pressed her knees down on the side, as he kneeled on the floor between her legs, her sex parading for him in all her splendour.

"Stay like this for me, my love."

He parted her folds, teasing those nether regions of hers, until his lips crashed on her pussy, and she shrieked.

As he tasted her through and through, sucking and licking, her fingers were in his hair. She fisted it as she thrashed about with her arousal, giving out little sounds of pleasure. She tried to close her legs, but his hands pushed them down to the side, wide, until his tongue burst inside her and made love to her. It wasn't long before she cried out with another orgasm that skyrocketed her into oblivion.

He stood and looked at her face while his fingers teased her until he exhausted her. He didn't let up.

Marcus tugged her to the centre of the bed, and he came down on her on all fours until he nestled between her thighs.

His cock inched inside her, in the wet, drenched, and throbbing wonderland that was her inner sanctum, and he homed in and out of her for some time, holding his pleasure until she was ready for him.

Soon, they both hit the spot in a delirium of endearments, and they crashed, worn out, on a tangled heap of limbs.

Sleep was not in his plan after what they had just done. He wanted her again, and he had her twice again that night. Their lovemaking enriched them until their bodies, satiated with love, drained, surrendered to a deep slumber.

Chapter 6

He opened his eyes, and the first thing he noticed was the divine sweep of velvety skin next to him. Erin looked magnificent; she was a dazzling vision. She was sleeping, in a seductive pose, propped up by pillows beside him. She was stark naked in all her glory, with her right arm raised and loose, draped over her head, with her left, elegant hand gingerly placed above her apex. Her lavish dark hair fell about her, framing her gorgeousness in contrast with her vast creamy expanse. Her plump bosom, a delectable sight of perfection, her twin peaks heaving. And oh, how he wished to lose himself in that wonderful valley of hers.

In that beguiling pose, Erin reminded him of an enticing painting he had once seen in the Old Masters Picture Gallery in Dresden, in Germany, while on honeymoon with his late spouse years ago.

Marcus and Penny had toured major cities in Europe with art galleries as their primary destination, like the one in Dresden, the Uffizi in Florence, the Prado in Madrid, the

Louvre in Paris, the National and the Portrait Galleries in London.

His late wife, Penny, God rest her soul, had been an artist and a painter. Marcus relished going around these museums with her. She was a fine art connoisseur, who could bring any canvas to life for him.

Of the countless paintings they had admired over the three-week tour, one mesmerised him above all others, the Sleeping Venus by Giorgione in Dresden, a masterpiece by one of the finest old masters of the Renaissance.

The sleeping Venus, dreaming of love, had entranced Marcus. He stood in front of the almost life-size female nude filling the pictorial frame in a backdrop much more than just a landscape, creating a harmonious unison that had stirred and shaken his very core. He stared at that large canvas for a good five minutes without moving, until his new wife had joked with him.

"Do you want to return to the hotel, my love? I'll lie down for you in the same manner of the lady in the portrait, in that precise position. So, you can feast your eyes on me," Penny whispered in his ear. As it happened, she never did.

Marcus smiled at the anecdote, bless her!

He didn't know why the painting attracted him besides the sheer beauty of it. That was until this very dawn as he stared at his new woman next to him. Perhaps the canvas evoked memories of her in his subconscious. A mirage of his youth, when he first met Erin, as he observed her at the regatta while she lay on the riverbank on a blanket, propped up by cushions... dressed, of course. In her pretty, flowery dress, in the wild recesses of his mind, the visions of her took a more alluring and arousing image.

Was Erin dreaming of love next to him now? He smiled at his foolishness and shook his head.

The beauty and erotic nature of the painting had stirred him, as Erin had aroused him, stretching on the riverbank that day long ago. Her body was forming a supple, curvaceous, and voluptuous image, as she was still stirring him right now next him in all her beauty.

Nothing covered her comeliness at that moment as he watched her. It gave a formidable pleasure to his senses. A purr of contentment left his lungs. It exposed her to him, and somehow, she seemed vulnerable and sensual. Suddenly, he felt he was intruding. He pulled the coverlet over her. Then he smiled and thought better of it.

After Penny died, he expected he would never be happy with a woman again. But now he hoped for the future.

The early morning was warm, and he uncovered her again. A small smile spread across his face as he looked at her and caressed her tummy with his fingertips. She rolled a hand over her stomach but didn't move from her position.

He tried to move cautiously. He didn't want to wake her up yet. Though, soon he would have to. She wouldn't like what he had to say, he was certain. What he would require of her.

For a few minutes, though, he wanted to enjoy the peace and admire her beauty, undisturbed. He wished to rejoice, watching her sleep in all her unrestrained loveliness. As he had delighted looking at her lying on the riverbank long ago.

Her long limbs, sinuous and shapely, suddenly turned and wrapped loosely around him. It brought a jolt to his heart. She allured him, and she was his now. She was his woman! God, the minx had utterly bewitched him from the dawn of time. She had beguiled him the moment he saw her fourteen years ago at the regatta, and she didn't even know it. Then he lost sight of her.

Now his good fortune had sent her back to him. For Marcus to heal her, or rather his sister to heal her, and for him to take care of her, to love her, to nurse her back to the blossoming flower he had seen that day on the riverbank. He would look after her, protect her. She belonged to him.

But she had that wild, unpredictable streak in her, and it wouldn't be easy. He would have to discipline the untamed side of her. She took his spanking well, too well, he would say… and he had enjoyed doing it. Bloody hell, she got so aroused by it, she climaxed through it, the minx. It made him laugh.

But for the next six weeks or so, she'd have to do what he told her, to the letter if they wished to succeed. Would she cooperate? He wasn't sure. He couldn't throw away a work of a lifetime, or that of family generations.

Marcus needed to pee, but he didn't want to raise her yet. So, he tried to shift his body from under her. She stirred as he removed her arm from him, and she turned the other way, but she didn't wake up. In all fairness, he had exhausted the spirited creature with his lovemaking.

For a first night together, he'd been demanding with her. She gave herself to him willingly. And God, she had pleased him, repeatedly. Hell, he would love nothing better than to be inside her right now, but he couldn't. It was daylight already. Though, after the party, the household would not awaken for hours.

As he moved to get out of bed, she moved too, and a waft of lavender reached his nostrils. Jesus! He adored her scent. He smelt the lavender on himself as he walked to the bathroom, and another smile graced his lips.

She was shy, but once you got to know her, she was lively, vibrant. He loved the spirited creature, but she would have to trust him. It was important that she believed in him, to have faith in him.

"Darling, wake up. Come on, sweetheart, time to get up," he said a few minutes later. He was wearing his boxers.

"Umm…" She spun the other way.

He laughed.

"Come on, Erin, you must rise." He sat on the side of the bed next to her. She opened her eyes, blinked, and then smiled languidly at him.

"Good morning, love." She draped her arms around his neck and pulled him to her. They kissed with tenderness.

"What time is it?" she mumbled, yawning when the kiss ended.

"Six am."

"Six? It's Sunday! What the hell?" she whined and sat up in the bed with a frown.

"Shush, you don't want to wake everybody, do you?" He brushed his thumb on her lips, and she kissed it.

"Umm… have you wakened me because you want me again, to love me…" She directed a mischievous and enticing little smile at him, fluttering her eyelids. He smiled and cocked his head. She pulled the waistband of his boxers, but he halted her hand with his.

"As much as I'd wish nothing else, no, darling," he said with a note of regret in his voice.

"No?"

"No." He shook his head as she stared at him.

"You don't want to make love to me?"

"Oh, I do! Trust me, I do. But we can't right now."

"No? Why not?"

"You must return to your bedroom before the household wakes up."

"My room?" she repeated. Her head drew back, incredulous at his words. Perhaps she hadn't heard him right.

"Yes, poppet, you must return to your room now." His face was grave but resolute.

"For heaven's sake, why?"

"Darling, it wouldn't do for you to be seen leaving my bedroom later. You must leave while everyone is asleep." He cupped her cheek and kissed her nose.

She slapped his hand off her face. "Why? God knows, I am not underage. I am single, you are a widower, so why not?"

"It is not as easy as that, my love," he said, shaking his head.

"I don't understand. What's the problem?" Her eyes grew enormous at him. He could see the disappointment in her eyes.

"Well, think of your reputation."

"My what?" she scoffed. "You are not serious!"

"I am, though."

"What reputation? Don't be ridiculous. We are two consenting adults who fancy the pants off each other. Those are Belinda's words, not mine." She laughed, and she moved her hands to pull his boxers down. He stopped her again, circling her wrist in his hand firmly.

"Please." This time his tone was more commanding. "Get dressed and return to your room."

"You *are* serious."

"I am."

"But who cares about my reputation? I want to stay here with you."

"Well, I care."

"Oh, don't be a fool, Marcus." She leapt out of the bed. Still naked, she gave him a contemptuous look, clearly annoyed. Then she stomped to the bathroom.

He admired her fabulous backside as it moved splendidly, still with a hint of redness crowning those spectacular long legs of hers. But she was in a huff as she shut the door with a bang.

He closed his eyes and inhaled. He knew she would not like it. Hell, he didn't like it, either, but he had no choice.

"You are sending me back to my room as if this was some sort of sordid little fuck. If so, at least have the decency to tell me the truth," she said when she returned from the bathroom, still naked, glaring at him, her hands on her hips.

"Put this on." He offered his party shirt to her. "I'm going to ignore your bad language because I upset you. But don't push me. Hurry, put this on. I can't have a reasonable conversation with you when you are starkers in front of me."

"I don't want to have a reasonable conversation. I want to make love to you!"

"Erin, please…"

She yanked the shirt from his hand and put it on then glared at him with thin lips.

"So, let's hear it."

"Sweetheart, we mustn't show our affection yet. Not for a while. I wish to keep this between us. We are in Zac's house, and I don't want to tell them. At least not yet."

"But why? Zac and Finley are my friends. They are yours, too. I got to know Mollie and Kathryn more since I'm convalescing at the clinic. They spent a lot of time visiting me during these months, and you know it. We have grown close despite our history. Even your sister said it was cleansing for me to overcome my troubled past with them and become friends, and we are. Why wouldn't we want to share this with them? Yesterday's dance thing with George at the party was Mollie's idea, you know, to entice you to me."

"Well, I never."

"It was her doing, we have…" She waved her hand between them in recollection of the night together.

"Good on her, darling! I must remember to buy her a nice present."

"Yes, you do that!"

"But Mollie doesn't realise exactly what happened after that, does she? And I don't wish her or anyone to know about us yet."

"Why? What's the harm? Of course, if you are not convinced about us, then tell me. I'll understand, but I thought you…"

"I am sure! I've never been so positive about anything in my life than I am about you and me. But you are a patient in my clinic, and I am a doctor. Though you are not my patient directly, it is my place, and I would not appreciate it if—"

"Oh, I get it! It is not my reputation then, is it? It is yours and your precious clinic! Certainly not mine. I wish you had just said that in the first place."

She looked for her dress. Erin yanked his shirt off herself, tossing it on the floor, none too pleased, and crammed her frock on as he spoke.

"Darling, listen to me, we must keep this to ourselves until we discharge you from the clinic, and then we can—"

"I get it!" And she walked to the door, opening it as she was about to leave. But he sprang from his seat, and in a second, Marcus grabbed her wrist, pulling her inside again.

He shut the door with his other hand. It rattled in the doorframe, making a noise he didn't intend to. But her behaviour frustrated him. He spun her and dragged her wrist behind her back, circling her waist with his arm.

Marcus crushed her against his chest, and she yelped with surprise. He mumbled a few dark curses.

She gasped. Erin picked up the furious expression in his eyes. She didn't realise what he was going to do.

But he seized her lips forcefully, with passion, ravishing her, showing his want, owning her.

"I forbid you to leave this room in this manner, in anger. Be grown up about this. I have given you my reasons, and you have to respect them. Trust me! My father worked himself to the ground for that clinic, and my grandfather gave life to it before him, and now it's mine. And as much as I need you, as much as I want you, I cannot let them down. Do you understand? Many lives depend on me, patients, and staff. I give work to most adults in the village. Besides, this is only for a short period, until Julia releases you from our care. Then, we can be free to be ourselves. To love each other," he said calmly.

She knew he was struggling to make it sound that way as the fire in his eyes betrayed his emotion. "Yes, I get it. You want your clinic much more than you want me," she murmured with trepidation. Though, there was defiance in her eyes and in her speech. It was a reproach to him. Her willful chin rose haughtily at him with disdain.

"You are behaving like a stubborn child. This has just earned you a spanking. I'll bank it for now as we have no time for it. Though, for the moment, you win." And he pulled her dress up to her waist, crushing his mouth to hers. His hands grabbed her bottom and dragged her up as he walked her back against the wall. He pressed her hard to the wall, and in one swift movement, his solid cock sunk deep inside her as she moaned and went limp in his arms, taking all of him in with joy.

Her insides melted in his muscular arms. His passion unleashed as he took strong possession of her, their bodies moving to the forceful rhythm of their love. His thrusts were deep and furious, and it took her to the edge in no time as they hit ecstasy. She moaned and whimpered when she reached the apex as she felt him filling her with his seed.

He kissed her, but now his lips were tender on her, lingering, delighting in her mouth. He drew out of her and released her back on her feet. Marcus drew her into a firm embrace. They stood silent for a time, their arms wrapped around each other, meditating about what had just happened.

"Stay there!" he commanded while she leaned on the wall and closed her eyes, still unable to speak. He went to the bathroom and returned with a towel. He lovingly cleaned her.

"Marcus, I-I—"

"You see what you do to me? You make me do things that no gentleman should do!"

"Darling, I'll take this anytime." She giggled, and he swatted her ass hard. She yelped.

He grabbed her upper arms and steadied her. "Look at me, Erin."

"Yes?" She raised her face to glance into his grey eyes, scorching her with the fire in them. She lowered hers. She was conscious she was about to hear what she didn't want to.

"Now, let's be clear. Today, we will behave as before. No hint of this to anyone," he said at last. He lifted her chin so he could look into her eyes.

"Not even to Mollie? She is my friend and—"

But he silenced her with another kiss. "Especially, not Mollie, do you understand? This is our secret. Here and at the clinic, not a word. Promise me!"

"Marcus, I—"

"Please..." he urged.

"Oh, all right, I promise. But only until I am released from your care, okay?"

"Deal!" He bit her lips playfully and pulled her dress down. She giggled in his mouth.

"And, Erin, never wear this silly little frock again! It is too bloody tempting." He moved to open the door. He glanced left to right in the hallway. Marcus swatted her backside out of the room. "Now go! And be good."

ERIN WENT TO HER ROOM, but it vexed her. She wished to shout her love for the man to the four winds. She wished her friends to know and to tease her. To congratulate her and partake in her joy. As it was, she'd have to wait ages for that, behave like nothing had changed. Marcus wanted it that way. She could understand his reasons, and though it made sense to her, she didn't like it. Not. One. Bit.

For a moment, she doubted him. How had he done this to her? If this was his intention, why make love to her then? It was his reputation and that of his precious clinic all along, not hers.

The bloody man! I could slap his face. He should have waited if this was how he felt.

Mind you, she didn't regret what happened between them. Even if he'd told her last night, before the event, she would have agreed to anything for one kiss, let alone the rest. But it hurt her. She understood the reasoning, but it didn't sit well with her.

Would she be able to endure weeks at the clinic without kissing him? Pretending that nothing transpired? Oh, God, it would be hell. She threw herself on the bed, exhausted from the lovemaking and with her horrid thoughts. She cried herself to sleep.

IT WAS early afternoon when people trickled down to the breakfast room after their deep sleep. Exhausted by the party and somewhat hungover, they gathered around the table. They looked the worse for wear.

Zac, Finley, Alex, and Marcus sat talking at one side, while Mollie, Kathryn, Clarissa, and Erin were at the other end of the table.

"You mean to say nothing happened between you and the doctor after the dance?" Mollie asked, drawing her brows together in disappointment.

"No!" Erin blushed, and she fidgeted with her cup of black coffee.

"It can't be."

"He just gave me an car full because I was drinking, that's all. Then I went to my room, alone."

"I don't believe it," her companion said. "He dragged you off the dance floor like a madman, when he saw you dancing with George in that red dress. I thought he was about to jump your bones." Mollie was trying to scrunch the truth out of her; she couldn't understand why her plan hadn't worked. She had witnessed Marcus's behaviour, and that was not a behaviour that induced to nothing.

"No, of course not. He is my doctor," she defended herself. She blinked rapidly.

"You are lying! And he is not your doctor."

"Oh, give it a rest, Mollie," Kathryn said, flicking her long hair back.

"No, I am not. I tell you, not a thing happened," Erin echoed, and she felt guilty at having to lie to her friend after the trouble she had gone through to make her plan work.

"But it can't be," her friend persisted. "I'm sure you were kissing on the landing."

"You are mistaken."

"Mollie, if the lady is telling you nothing happened, it is true. Why would she lie to us? Why do you find it so hard to believe! Alex flirted with me all night, but I made it back to my room alone. Damn man! When I would gladly have... well, I mean, your mother has my daughter, Mia... Whatever!" Clarissa huffed. "These are men for you. Let the girl be. If she said nowt happened, then it's true."

The girls whispered to avoid the men at the other end hearing their conversation.

Erin was glad Mollie stopped grilling her about Dr. Stewart, though her companion peered at her through her nose, not quite convinced. She wasn't sure how much more she could have taken of this probing.

Erin glanced furtively at the other side, but Marcus didn't look her way once. She felt disheartened.

WHEN MID-AFTERNOON CAME, Marcus announced they were returning to the clinic immediately rather than in the morning as planned.

It disappointed his companions, the same for the girls, but it didn't surprise them. The nature of his job was unpredictable, even on a Sunday, in particular with a clinic at full capacity.

He asked Erin to pack her bags and get ready to leave.

If his friends were disappointed, she was beyond upset for words. It wrecked her.

She had counted on devoting another night to Marcus in Mollie's house. She thought to sneak in his room in the dead of night and stay with him. But it wasn't to be.

She knew, once they returned to the clinic, it would be awfully difficult to spend time together. With so many people around, between staff and patients, she realised it was quite impossible. Besides, Marcus had made it clear he would not jeopardise his position or that of the clinic for her.

Though she made no reply, she did not let her frustration show. She packed her things; they said their goodbyes to their friends and set off.

The drive was quiet and rather sombre. He sensed her sorrow.

Erin sat in the passenger seat of his open-roofed convertible, silent and rigid like a statue. She looked ahead as he drove them back to the clinic, as if nothing had happened. She didn't ask him why he had changed his plans, why they were going back now instead of in the morning. She avoided glancing at him, or speaking, fearing she would burst into tears. Only the incessant twirl of a ring on her finger and her stillness betrayed her uneasiness and her mood, not to mention the painful tightening in her chest that was crushing her.

Marcus turned into a long country lane, away from the main road. She glanced at him, but she didn't ask, thinking it was just a shortcut to the clinic he had taken. Only when he parked in the courtyard of a boutique hotel in the Cotswolds, in a huge, gated estate, did her eyes become as big as the moon, not daring to believe it. She stared at him.

"Good. I'll pick up the bags from the boot of the car and check-in." He had a tiny grin on his face.

It was then, his intentions were apparent to her. Her squeals of delight reverberated around the courtyard.

"Shush, Erin." An enormous smile of pleasure slowly formed on his lips.

She flung her arms around his collar and smothered his face in kisses as a sonorous laugh left his mouth.

He craved for a romantic, sultry night of lovemaking with her far from all prying eyes before returning to the clinic in the morning.

Chapter 7

The magnificent hotel sat in the heart of the Cotswolds, in the depths of the Gloucestershire countryside. It was set in a bucolic rural setting that made her cry with joy; it was so pretty.

The hotel, formerly an old coaching-inn in days bygone, was elegant. The original house dated back to the 14th century, with stunning areas and rich in history. It kept its rustic charms, with large stone fireplaces in many of the public and private rooms. It boasted vaulted beamed ceilings and antique furniture.

"Sweet Jesus, this must be expensive. You didn't have to do this." Erin's lips quivered, and she placed a hand on her heart as they entered the suite he had booked. The suite had beautiful, quirky period features with original paintings. Her eyes became misty. She kissed his cheek coyly.

He laughed. Seeing her emotion, he caressed her hair. He felt guilty at having upset her that morning with his sudden request. "Glad you like it, sweetheart." Marcus circled her waist, drawing her to him and kissing her nose.

"It's lovely, Marcus, thank you!"

"I have asked a lot of you, Erin, wanting to keep our relationship a secret, I know. It's going to be even harder once we are at the clinic, and I thank you for being so understanding and respecting my wishes," he went on and his lips crashed on hers, ravishing her.

"Ooh…" she mumbled in his mouth.

"Is there a bedroom?" she asked when the kiss ended. She raised her eyebrows with a naughty smile on her face.

He chuckled. "A bedroom? Um… " He tapped his chin in mock pensiveness, but his grey eyes had darkened. He ambled, as if not sure there was one, glancing this way and that way around the suite, in a pretend search for it, in jest.

She giggled and followed him until he enticed her into the bedroom. A massive, canopied bed was a key feature, and the room was complete with its own private terrace.

"Tonight, I want you all to myself," he said as his head made a quick movement towards the bed.

"Oh, Marcus, you are adorable!" She guffawed, and he raised a brow at her with a dubious expression.

"Adorable? Not sure about that, but I hope this goes some way to make amends. When Dr. Devlin releases you from the clinic, we'll have many such nights. I promise you, my love." More kisses took her breath away.

"I'll keep you to your word. You'll regret having said that." She laughed when they stopped kissing.

The huge, canopied bed was soon introduced to their passionate lovemaking, but hunger beckoned them. They went out to explore the place.

The hotel guestbook over the years was impressive, ranging from princes, old and new, to dignitaries, to film stars who had vacationed there. The receptionist told her that Liz Taylor and Richard Burton had once stayed there. Given what she was up to with Marcus, she thought the passionate spirit of the famous couple lingered around the place and rubbed off on them, Erin felt so close to him.

There was a spa in a secluded and tranquil corner of the hotel. They made a mental note to visit it in the morning. They were hungry, but first he needed an apéritif.

. Tucked away at the rear of the restaurant, the seductively lit bar had a speakeasy atmosphere.

It amazed Marcus that the bar included many boozy botanical beverages. Its signature drink was a Lavender Negroni, which he immediately ordered, as lavender reminded him of Erin's scent. It was a mixture of gin, Vermouth Rosso, Campari and lavender apéritif. It had an ornamental floral sprig to top it. He let her have a sip of it, and she deemed it heavenly, while she had a non-alcoholic drink.

It seemed to him all his senses were partaking of Erin. Marcus set his eyes on her. She was radiant, glowing. In a demure, beautiful flowery summer dress, she looked divine. His hand was caressing her, touching the smooth, pearly softness of her arm. His nose never missed her flowery, exhilarating lavender scent, now mingled with another perfume.

Her mellifluous voice floated to his ears, like a sweet melody of notes, titillating him. She was telling him the way Mollie had concocted the plan to bring them together, making him laugh. His booming laughter was manly, and he noticed it prickled her skin.

Drinking the cocktail that tasted and smelled of lavender, Marcus was consumed by her, a complete fill to his senses and a joy to his heart. He beamed, and he couldn't help putting a hand behind her neck and drawing her to him to steal a quick kiss. Her eyes were large and awe-struck with love for him.

It was time for dinner, though, and they were starving. The restaurant was within a grand hall, added to the building in the 16th century. But the sleek marble tables and laid-back leather seats gave the place a modern feel and tone to it. Erin ordered veal cutlets, while he had a Chateaubriand steak cooked medium-rare.

Marcus chose an aged Barolo Riserva red wine to go with his meal.

Barolo was one of Marcus's favourite wines, and that particular one, an exquisite vintage. That night, the wine seemed to resemble his girl. If he were to compare it with a person, it would be to a shy woman, like Erin was timid on the surface. When his nose approached the wine, it greeted him with delicate floral smells with crimson fruits, light, intoxicating, like her scent. Then he tasted the wine, full-bodied, ample and the harsh tannins in it showed up on his palate and he figured out the personality of this wine, like he understood Erin's rounded nature, vulnerable at times, strong at others, and when she felt comfortable with someone, she sparkled.

It took time and patience to approach her. The best of fourteen years, he would suggest. And just like the aged wine, she became addictive once he experienced its delicious flavour. He had become addicted to Erin the second she had landed in his clinic. Or dare he say from the instant he saw her at the regatta?

Yes, she was his Barolo wine, sultry, delicious, full-on, red-hot, addictive, and intoxicating.

As he enjoyed his wine that night, it was like sipping her. Facing him at the table with the loveliest smile on her sweet lips, he enjoyed every minute with her as she sipped on her sparkling water.

They took their time with supper. They talked about everything and nothing. They got comfortable with each other, laughing, and joking. Following the romantic dinner, they went for a walk around the grounds on that wonderful August evening.

It was a stellar night. Bright stars glittered in the dark inky sky, beckoning them with their twinkle. The half-moon hypnotised them, beaming with reddish hues. It seemed to lure love out of their hearts to flow freely and with tenderness encircle the other, like magic hands enveloping them. So, it was. They responded to the mood of the night and the expanse of the universe. It took their breath away.

The air felt fresher in the countryside. There was a cool breeze, and he put his jacket over her summery dress, keeping her warm. They walked hand-in-hand like young lovers, laughing and relishing each other's company until they returned to their room.

Chapter 8

As they entered the suite, he brushed his lips on hers. His hands roamed over her body as he kissed her unhurriedly, savouring her mouth. He locked the door without breaking the kiss and unzipped her dress, letting it float down to the floor. Then he scooped her up into his arm as she squealed with joy, moved to the bedroom, and laid her down on the bed.

"Do not move, darling," he said, caressing her face. "I'll be with you in a moment."

She lay on her side, her chin propped up by her hand. Erin watched him with a smile.

His eyes, with a mischievous glint, never left hers as he undressed himself, leaving his boxers on. He went to the dressing table. He perused through the items there. Marcus clutched a bottle of scented lotion. He smelled the contents and nodded, satisfied.

"Tonight, sweetheart, I am giving you a massage." He raised an eyebrow with meaning, and she giggled. He dimmed the lights and opened a package on the dressing stand. Marcus took the wax candles and lit them. He positioned them around the room and brought two to the bedside tables.

She glanced at him from the canopied bed. She inhaled the air; it had a pleasing, seductive floral fragrance.

He had asked the hotel reception for those items beforehand, and they delivered them while they were at dinner. He wanted to surprise her. The candles, adding to the ambience, helped him create the mood. He uncorked a bottle of champagne, handing her a flute.

"Cheers, Erin," he said and sipped. She did too, but after only two sips, he took her drink from her hands. He placed both glasses on the table. "Ready?"

"Ah, I adore massages, Marcus. The candles have a gorgeous perfume; this is lovely." She clapped her hands excitedly. No man had ever done anything like this for her.

"Good! On your tummy, sweetheart." He came over to her.

She giggled, and her eyes gleamed in anticipation. Once she turned over, he straddled her, but kept his weight on his knees.

He moved her hair from her back and undid her bra, removing it to free her breasts.

Her arms crossed under her face as she lay on her front, her profile showing.

He leaned over and kissed her nose. He opened the bottle of lotion and poured a few drops on the silky skin of her back. The cool lotion on her warm skin made her squeal with delight, and she wriggled.

"Do not move, poppet, stay still." He scooped some of it and rubbed it on his hands. He grazed her nape with the pads of his fingertips, following the smooth curves of her neck and shoulders. Then he let his palms glide across her frame. The first touches were long, lingering, and purposeful.

She moaned; it felt so wonderful.

He kneaded her skin, applying a tiny pressure on her shoulders. He followed the contours of her body sinuously, her natural shape, his thumbs moving in little circles, soothing, and smoothing her.

Another moan left her mouth. "Oh, that's marvellous."

"Good, my love." He brushed his lips on her neck, and she whimpered in anticipation.

"Marcus…" she moaned with a puff of air.

The fine sweeps of his hands resumed over her shoulders, advancing down towards her lower back with great sensual strokes. He splashed more lotion into his palms and over her skin, and another puff of air left her mouth. He took his time, pleasuring her with the rub.

Her pussy ignited as his palms moved over her body, unhurriedly, with enticing caresses. Her body felt smooth, aroused, and on fire. It was as if she were in Heaven and angels were caressing her with feathers. He focused on her delightful shoulder and inviting back, all the way down, then winding up with her arms. Marcus stepped to one side. He drew her right arm in his hands and massaged her upper arm gingerly with slow strokes. Then, her forearm, ending with her hand and long fingers, one by one. He put her index finger in his mouth and sucked it.

She groaned; her pussy pulsated. Then, he turned to her left arm. On her other side, he rubbed and kneaded through to her pure pleasure. He straddled her again, and he pushed her hair aside so he could caress her earlobe between his thumb and forefinger, tracing the lining of the ear.

"Marcus…" There was a note of need in her voice as her clit throbbed.

He moved down, brushing his tongue from her nape, down all the way to her lower back as his hands followed suit working on her. It made her shudder.

He got rid of her panties. He kneaded and rubbed each buttock, caressing them as more lotion cascaded over her skin. A few gentle smacks grazed her backside too.

She hissed. By then she was squirming under him, her lips letting out little moans and soft cries of his name.

He had a wicked smile on his face, relishing the power he had over her, enjoying the touch of her silky, pearly skin. His manhood was as hard as a rod.

Her body was limp and easy in his expert hands. He was a master at this. What a revelation. Her master! Erin wouldn't want it any other way.

Marcus used his creative streak. He considered ways to make the massage as sensual as possible. His teeth pinched her backside with tiny nibbles on it and she rocked her bottom. He had her moaning like no tomorrow as his tongue and hands caressed her inner thighs languidly down to her feet. Butterflies rolled in her tummy; her wet channel tightened and was doing clenching exercises. She couldn't say how much more she could take of this. It was a sinful, hypnotising, divine torture. Her pussy was glistening in anticipation.

He whispered sweet things into her ear, his bass tone purring to her in a sexy sing song.

"Marcus… please," she pleaded. She craved release; she was ready. Her throat was dry.

He would have fucked her there and then, but he carried on. This was about her, not about him. He wished this to be memorable for her, to last as long as possible. So, he held back, even though it was tormenting him, too. But the night was young. He had all the time in the world. Tonight, she was his and his alone.

He spun her around to face him. He nuzzled her cheeks and his lips brushed hers, stealing a deep kiss. He proceeded with the same attention and care to massage the front of her body, from her neck, where he kissed her soft spot down to her breasts. He kneaded her bosom, cupping each round perfect mountain, pinching the pink tips. Then, he sucked and licked them as she cried out little sounds of pleasure. With each caress, with each stroke and rub of her body, he was saying to her, *I adore you, and you are mine.*

"Marcus, please…" she moaned her desire, but he smiled at her and continued his amorous, sensual torture beyond her belly button. He kissed and massaged her all over with the lotion, and when he arrived at her erogenous zone, she glanced at him in need.

Moving his thumbs closely, one after the other, he gave her a rolling sensation over her flat, creamy tummy down to her apex. She was too aroused for any consequential thought. He tortured her with his passion. Her sight focused on him, begging him to take her, while his devilish smile told her *not yet!* He sucked her clit and lapped up her drenched folds with his tongue.

She hissed as she thrashed about, but his firm hands kept her still and pressed down. She wished to be out of her misery, but he had other ideas.

He left her for a moment.

She opened her eyes wide, staring at the ceiling, wondering what he was doing, not having the strength to look around, somewhat limp on the bed. She widened her arms and fisted the sheets in her hands.

He went to the large sunken bath and turned the taps on, filling the bathtub with scented salts.

"Darling..." she called out, her body heaving, her mind in the clouds, dazed, waiting, and desiring him like she had never craved a man before him.

When the tub was filled, he scooped her up into his arms, kissing her, before placing her in it. He dispensed of his boxers and entered the bath too, sitting in it behind her.

She placed her head on his chest, and he wrapped his arms and legs around her. His hands glided down over her breasts smoothly, gingerly, until they found his way to her pussy. His fingers played with her folds to his heart's content as she moaned little cries of joy, until they thrust inside her. He pleasured her, teasing her, giving her delight. She was too aroused to last long. She climaxed on his fingers in a blaring hiss soon enough.

He wrapped his arms around her and held her in the bath for a while in the warm scented, bubbly water. Then he bathed her like a baby. His soapy palms roamed her body back and forth, lingering in all the right places, over soft peaks and vast valleys, not leaving a single inch of skin untouched. She was soon under his spell again, ready for him.

She sighed with little cries, pleading repeatedly with him until he turned her over him. She straddled him. His enormous hands gripped her hips, raising her so she could slide down on his substantial erection. He needed to be careful, or he wouldn't last a minute, having controlled himself for so long.

Erin moaned and purred, as he buried his cock deep between her thighs. He stayed there for a few moments, not moving, completely still, having his fill of her, deep inside her, relishing her tight little pussy clenching all around on him. A guttural groan left his mouth and burst into the room. Then he began to move with deep, forceful thrusts. She arched her back, but he held her firmly on him as he slammed his cock inside her, over and over, until he took them both out of their misery to a crescendo of ecstasy.

That night Marcus loved her long and hard, in and out of the water. He couldn't have enough of her. He did delicious things to her body in the bath, in the bed, and somewhere in between. He did some things with his tongue he knew she liked from the previous night. He did some things with his cock she had never done, and she learned to enjoy them too.

"God, almighty! I feel like a new woman," she blurted out at one point after a powerful orgasm had taken them both drifting in pure, unadulterated fevered passion, and he roared with laughter, kissing her, and tickling her until she almost peed.

"Are you, poppet?"

"Aha, my cobwebs are gone forever after this."

"Cobwebs?"

"Oh, never mind, it's a long story. I'll tell you someday."

They were enamoured. So, that night, he made slow, tender love to her. At times, he possessed her with fervent devotion, roughly, hard and fast, and they did it several times. He brought her to the heights of passion, every time as if it was their first.

While her love-struck eyes were doing the talking, telling him the story, his soul leaped and bounced with a flaming fever for his woman.

Marcus watched her fall asleep in his arms. He exhausted her with the exciting weekend and his demanding lovemaking. She was spent with bliss and utterly his.

———

THE NEXT DAY they rose early. They headed straight for the spa in a secluded corner of the hotel and had a dip in the pool. Marcus made love to her there and then, too. But Erin resisted his advances, her shy nature fearing that someone would walk in on them and she would die of shame.

"What about your reputation then, hey?" she said, raising a brow to him. "Um…"

"You sweet poppet!" He laughed.

"No, I don't think so, you lover-man," she chided playfully.

They headed back to the room for a shower and breakfast on their private terrace overlooking the grounds.

The boisterous mood had cooled down after they made love in the bedroom, perhaps too aware of the lovely weekend ending and asking themselves when they would spend such a wonderful time again.

The conversation became quieter. They both knew they had to return to the clinic, and things would be different there. She promised him she would respect his wishes of keeping their love a secret. So, their attitudes became sombre. It was time for them to head for the car. With a last walk on the grounds, they committed to memory every detail of the place and the passion shared.

This night would have to last them for the foreseeable future.

Chapter 9

It had been two weeks since Erin and Dr. Stewart returned to the clinic from their amorous weekend. Except for one afternoon three days later, when he kissed her fortuitously in his office, Erin had not spoken to him or seen him other than at meals times. Even then, he hardly gave her a cursory glance as they sat at separate tables.

She shared her mealtime with her friends as usual, with Belinda Waltham, Lily Banks and Goran Marshall, with whom she had formed a close bond while there; Dr. Stewart seated with his staff instead. They acted as if nothing happened.

He kept his distance, as he had warned her. He hardly spoke to her other than a swift good morning or goodnight or such in her general direction, when she was with her companions.

Marcus had stressed to her again, as he drove them back to the clinic following their night at the hotel, that they had to maintain their distance. Their romance must stay a secret, keeping their liaison to themselves. "Nobody must know," he had warned her.

She was even forbidden to tell her friends.

"You mustn't, Erin, I don't want Belinda or Lily gossiping."

"But why? They are very discreet," she asked with a pout, crossing her arms over her chest. Feeling more at ease with him, she felt she could protest this.

"It wouldn't do to show ourselves, in particular, with patients or staff. I have explained already why. You are to say, as you did at Mollie's, that nothing happened if they ask. You are a patient in my clinic, Erin. Even if I am not your doctor directly, it would not be appropriate. We have to continue as we were until we release you from our care. It won't be long now, darling. But until that day, we have to act as if nothing happened. We have to protect our reputations. Mine, the clinic, and yours! You must do as I say," he commanded peremptorily, seeing her more argumentative on the issue and dismissing any further discussion on the matter.

"My reputation is laughable. What you really mean is your reputation and that of your clinic. That's what you care about, not me."

"I refuse to explain this again. We have been through this several times. Keep silent on our relationship, end of story!" Marcus was cross with her for insisting. He refused to be brought into the same argument.

She had understood the reason, the necessity of it, but disappointment crashed in on her. She didn't know what she was expecting after the weekend of passion they spent together. He'd frozen her out of this conversation, not wanting to be dragged into it once more.

The closer they got to the clinic that morning, the cooler he became, and she complained, not mincing her words. "You are selfish," she spat.

"Don't be such a baby. I don't want to repeat it, Erin. But this is how it is going to be." Though, he had stopped the car and kissed her divinely, somewhat appeasing her.

Now, two weeks down the line at the clinic, this distance between them was upsetting her. Seeing him about and not being able to speak to him, not touch him or kiss him, was driving her insane. He had cancelled two of her weekly appointments, too, which had sent her into a downward spiral of emotions.

It was unbearable; she was in a living hell. She didn't realise it was going to be so difficult for her. Worst of all, she was doubting him now. She suspected he didn't care about her. It had just been a sexual thirst for him. It meant zilch to him. *A dirty weekend. The loathsome playboy!* He changed his mind. His reputation was too valuable to him to taint it with the likes of her, with a messed-up woman who people in his standing would shun and make fun of behind her back. He had second thoughts. She was sure of it. She convinced herself he had no intention of taking things any further. A convenient pretence, but that weekend had meant nothing to him but sex.

In the light of day, he's realised he made a mistake, she tortured herself. *I am a complete mess of a woman, and he is an eminent doctor, I don't fit into his life. He wants nothing to do with me.*

Who the hell cared about her reputation, anyway! No one gave a damn about it, least of all herself. No, what he worried about was *his* reputation and that of his precious clinic's. That was the truth... She had turned into a meaningless obstacle to his way to glory, and he had to keep her quiet somehow, to protect himself. She was on tenterhooks torturing herself with this. She'd cried herself to sleep the last few nights, feeling miserable.

Her friend, clever as ever, had grasped a change in her, and she was curious. "Come on, Erin, you can tell me. I won't say a word. Did anything happen with the doctor at the party? You seem so preoccupied, kind of depressed, too. Besides, you have told me nothing exciting. Did he, you know... Why was Dr. Stewart so determined to leave Goran behind at the clinic? It makes no sense. Goran is your bodyguard after all," Belinda persisted.

"Oh, Bella, give over."

"I am sure Dr. Stewart has the hots for you. These days he doesn't look at you as much as he used to, which makes me suspect him more. Something happened! Oh, do tell! Spill the beans," her friend teased her while she blushed scarlet.

"There is nothing to tell. We had two dances, that's all. I fooled around with a young chap, though. Quite good-looking, he was. He was an incredible dancer," Erin replied, describing the way she had danced with George and the dress Mollie had given her, to displace the attention from Marcus and herself. She pretended she liked George more than she had, to divert the spotlight from her man.

"He owns all of this, you know, the doctor, I mean." Belinda dismissed her story with a wave of her hand. "He is quite a catch. Fergus, my older brother, invited him to our country estate for a weekend a long time ago, after his wife died and before my prison palaver exploded. He was trying to match us up. Though very handsome, Dr. Stewart is not my type. Anyway, my prison issues soon thwarted any thoughts my brother had on matching us." Belinda snorted.

"I see." Erin gulped, her tongue stuck to her palate. A shiver ran through her. Her friend's statement emphasised it. She was right. Erin was not good enough for Marcus. If the wealthy sister of an earl was not good enough for him because of her minor problems with the law, Erin, a nobody who had more problems than one could count, not half as pretty or young as Belinda, wouldn't cut it. No! She wouldn't!

"I am surprised no one has snapped him up yet, maybe because Dr. Stewart is a pain in the ass," her friend observed.

"Darling, give over—" Lily said, directing a small smile towards her friend.

"You'd better hurry if you wish to land him. He's been a widower for over two years. There are a lot of women swarming around him. There are too many pretty nurses. Be quick off the mark if you want him. Umm… did something happen at the party? I won't tell, I promise," Belinda insisted with a naughty glint in her eyes.

"Stop, please, or I am sitting somewhere else. Nothing happened! How many times do I have to say it? God, Dr. Stewart is like an army sergeant. A despot! No, thank you. You are right; he is handsome but a pain in the backside. The pretty nurses are welcome to him," Erin said with a heavy sigh, and at that moment she meant it.

She was thinking of him as if he were a dictator. He had forbidden her to say anything to her friends, imposing on her a distance from him that was killing her. She couldn't bear it. She dismissed Belinda's innuendos. Her companion was fishing for information, and she tried to avoid it the best she could. Though, Erin became more irritated with

Marcus and with herself. She was vexed at herself because she had been careless and let her guard down with this guy.

She should have known better than to mess with this man. Yet, Marcus had seemed so genuine during the weekend they spent together. He was so loving, in particular at the hotel. She had a wet dream three nights ago, where he was roasting her backside again, and she had an orgasm while asleep, dreaming about it. She awakened, drenched.

Dear Lord, if my head was in shambles when I came here, now it is worse. I'll end up with a broken heart, too.

She was suffering; she got frustrated with him, doubting Marcus and his motives for keeping this quiet. She needed to understand if he'd changed his mind. If so, better he told her this minute than linger in this inferno of uncertainty a moment longer. Erin had to know either way. She had gone to Nurse Stevenson, who guarded his diary of appointments, asking for one.

"I am sorry, Miss Blake, but Dr. Stewart's diary is full for this week. Let see how next pans out," the young nurse responded.

Lily made an appointment that day. So why couldn't she have one? Had he given instructions not to let her in? Could that be possible? Was he avoiding her? Erin concluded, yes, he was!

If he thinks he'll dismiss me, reject me, without having the guts to tell me to my face, he has another think coming, she resolved.

"I'll see you later, girls," Erin said as she rose from the table as soon as they finished dinner.

Dr. Stewart had already left the dining room. She knew he worked until late in his office often, so she hoped to find him there.

"Where are you going?" Goran asked, "Shall I come with you?"

"No," she cried out. Goran's watching over her was quite lax now, given she had been in the clinic for months, causing no trouble. But he insisted on accompanying her around most of the time with his sweetheart in tow. These days, Lily and Goran were attached at the hip. They went everywhere together. She wondered, if once Lily returned to her actress' life on the outside, if this passion of theirs would last in the real world, like hers and Dr. Stewart's had not lasted more than a weekend. Not on her part… but for the doctor, it was just a sexual dalliance.

Blast! So, right now, she had a pressing love life to sort out… one way or another!

"Where are you going then?" he repeated, looking at her when he had no reply.

"I need to speak to Dr. Stewart, something about my therapy, nothing to worry about. Dr. Devlin said I should ask him."

"Shall I come with you?" He cocked his head on one side, not entirely sure she was okay.

"No, Goran, seriously."

"Fine, we'll be in the reading room when you are done."

AS SHE WALKED with purpose towards his office, she had an impulse to have some fresh air. She needed it. She was getting hot, more through her agitation than anything else. Erin couldn't breathe. She opened the French doors in the hallway and stepped outside into the gardens.

She inhaled and closed her eyes. It was an early evening in September as twilight set. The weather was lovely. The unbearable heat of a few weeks ago had ceased as the season prepared for a change, thus providing a mellow, delightful, warm dusk.

As the day gave way to the night, there was a rising moon, soaring large in the sky. As the dark shadows of the east began to coat the blue mantle and the land, the stars shimmered and flickered over the sublime landscape. With the hubbub of day coming to a close, the countryside's nocturnal world was taking centre stage. She heard the tweet call of the owl, a prelude to its song, a strange hooting, wheezing whoop, "Hoo."

Erin got used to it through the months. Frogs and toads in the pond were vociferous too, with their rapping and croaking noises, and the whole night life awakened to create its nighttime melody.

The clinic was in the Cotswolds, in a charming spot in the English countryside, in the county of Worcestershire. She had enjoyed the views from its elevated position during the months; it was splendid, so calming. She knew the area well.

From where she stood in the garden, in the darkening twilight, she set her eyes on the green, gently rolling hills of outstanding natural beauty surrounding the place. The landscape was idyllic. It spread far and wide all around. The soothing view gave her some peace to her torment and strength for her purpose. It was a beautiful part of the country.

Her eyes rejoiced, her soul sang, and calmed her somewhat despite her distressing thoughts on him. She inhaled the warm breeze. It appeased her. She relaxed for a while. It lulled her. Suddenly, she didn't feel as if she were about to battle. Her heart mellowed.

If Marcus didn't desire her anymore, no harm done, she considered soberly. She'd enjoyed the sex. *Bloody hell, their lovemaking…* She got wet just by thinking about it. She suspected she would never be turned on by a man in this way again. She never knew she could be aroused by a man spanking her. *God! The mind-blowing sex…* She would miss it!

That memory would have to suffice. She was a grown woman. At thirty-three, things happened. She would take it. She would be brave! Besides, better to find out sooner rather than later if he was done with her. Before she got too attached to him. Erin wished to know. She must! She could not stand the uncertainty any longer.

During these past two weeks, doubts had assailed her. Her insecurities played havoc in her mind. She needed to know. It was human to doubt, and she doubted his motives for the secrecy. Was his all a hoax?

Who am I kidding? I may be strong in accepting it, but it will hurt like hell if he doesn't want me.

She gulped a good intake of air to give herself courage. Erin walked around the gardens for a few minutes to clear her head. She wanted Marcus more than anything in the world. The problem was he didn't want her. She believed it; she was just another patient to him, one of many.

She sat on the root of a gigantic oak tree, leaning back against its mighty trunk, and closed her eyes to think. A tear stained her cheek, and she wiped it with her hand. Erin loved

Marcus. In her uncertain world, this was the only certainty. She would accept whatever he decided, even if it destroyed her soul. His behaviour implied he could do without her with no effort at all. He looked his usual composed and controlled person, going about his business like she didn't exist. She was sure he didn't love her. If he resisted two weeks with not a word to her, not as much as a smile to her, then he didn't want her. *Well, there* was *that one kiss. No, he couldn't possibly love her,* she tormented herself.

His excuse was their reputations, but she believed he had changed his mind. It was as simple as that; he had no need for her. All he wanted was his precious clinic, his career.

She opened her eyes and swung to look at the magnificent house. It had been once Marcus's family home until his grandfather tuned it into a clinic. Pristine lawns surrounded the mansion. The house stood tall and stately over the landscape, a Tudor manor with huge, cased windows. Impressive, striking and somewhat intimidating, the building was like its principal, like Dr. Stewart. It didn't strike her as a clinic at all; it had the look of a grand country estate.

Erin realized, over the months, why it was so pricey. The medical care was first class, the personnel competent, sympathetic, and smart. And its owner, Dr. Stewart, was a prominent doctor who was respected and admired in his profession. That's why he had no reason to want her, a hot mess, feeble-headed woman. He would probably be ashamed of her.

No! Why she thought this would work was beyond her. Though if she had to be honest, right now, Marcus was not in her good books. Not. At. All.

Erin walked towards the freshly cut lawns. She could smell the grass that had been trimmed that day. She liked this majestic mansion, in this wonderful spot of the countryside.

Her spirits rose, despite the turmoil raging in her heart and mind, and she sighed. Whatever happened next, it would appease her to know where she stood with him, so she could move on and get on with her life. Time to find out what the rules-mongering doctor had in mind for her.

SHE RETURNED TO THE HOUSE. She followed the path in the hallway until she reached the other side of the building then made her way to the anteroom. The waiting area had soft, bright armchairs, but it was empty that evening. A counter faced the massive oak door to his office with a placard that said "Dr. Stewart" on it.

Nurse Stevenson stayed at the desk in the waiting area to usher his calendar of appointments in and out. But there was nobody there then. Perhaps the pretty girl had gone home.

Erin put her ear to the door. There were voices coming from his office, but the heavy oak muffled them. She wished she could hear what they were saying and pondered who was inside with Marcus.

She sat for a minute, wondering what to do. Should she wait? Whoever it was wouldn't stay long with the doctor, not at this hour. She remained there and shuffled in the armchair for a moment or two. She was anxious, uncertain how to proceed or what to expect. She wasn't even sure what she would say to him exactly.

Dear God, she had not prepared herself too well for this. Her insecurities had carried her away and made her panic, but she could not backtrack now. She needed to know where she stood. She wished to hear it from the horse's mouth. What he felt for her, come what may.

She could not live in this limbo any longer. It was killing her.

She peered about in the waiting area. It was a pleasant room, a little dark at this time of evening, but flooded with light during the day.

She sighed. She made her mind up; she would wait. Though her heart almost stopped when she heard footsteps. Erin glimpsed into the hallway and saw Stevenson. The nurse was returning to her desk, and she had to make a split-second decision. The young girl would not allow her in or to wait for him. She struggled with herself for a moment.

"Miss Blake?" Stevenson called out as she approached the room. "What are you doing here?"

"I need to see the doctor," she mumbled.

Damn! In, now. Go, woman, go! Erin thought to herself.

"You can't, it's late. He is—"

She took action.

DR. STEWART AND HIS SISTER, Dr. Devlin, were deep in conversation. They were catching up with the events of the day. As they were talking, the door to his office flung open. Erin paused in the doorframe for an instant, enough for her to scan the room, then she swiftly marched inside.

"Miss Blake!" Marcus stood from his chair. The dark look in his eyes revealed a story, and his expression said *I'm not pleased with the interruption.*

Nurse Stevenson followed her in. "I am sorry, doctor, but I told Miss Blake... I couldn't stop her," she said apologetically.

Dr. Stewart glanced, bewildered, from one to the other.

"Forgive me, D-Doctor, but it is important I-I speak to you," Erin stammered, wringing her hands with a penitent look on her face.

"Are you all right, Miss Blake?" Dr. Devlin asked her, standing from her seat, moving close to her. The young doctor patted her back reassuringly with her hand.

"Yes, yes, I am fine, but I must speak to Dr. Stewart. Now," Erin blabbered on before she lost her nerve, but she turned as red as a beetroot.

"I understand," his sister said as she glanced at Marcus and then at Miss Blake. A knowing little smile formed on her lips, directed at her brother, a hint of amusement in Dr. Devlin's eyes.

He sighed, irritated, and then scowled at Erin. Marcus launched a hard stare at her. If he'd been able to throw arrows from his eyes, she would be in a heap on the floor, dead. He looked at his watch; it was late. He tapped his wristwatch with his fingers, showing his impatience in no uncertain terms.

"Okay, you run along. I'll handle this. You can go home, Stevenson, and I'll see you later, Julia," he stated curtly, moving around his desk and hurrying the two women out of the room.

"Are you sure you don't want me to stay, Marcus?" his sister asked him, with a twinkling expression in her eyes.

"No!" he barked. As he closed the door in her face, he heard a bubble of laughter coming from the other side.

He grumbled a curse under his breath. Then he turned to her.

"I am sorry to barge in, but I..." Erin mumbled under his deadly scrutiny, and she shifted on her feet. She gulped. At that moment, she wasn't certain she was doing the right thing anymore.

"What the hell is wrong with you? Didn't we agree that—" he began, his tone harsh, unyielding.

It was then, her irritation with him flooded her blood and billowed out of her. She rose to the occasion, venting out her frustration. "Heavens, no! No, Doctor. *You* agreed. I had no choice! *You* decided this, not me. Yes, you did. And you don't even have the guts to tell me to my face. It was just sex for you, wasn't it? A bit of a dirty weekend, nothing more. Admit it!"

"Dear God! Keep your voice down, you silly girl."

"Silly?"

"Damn right, you are."

"It was sex you were after. That's all you wanted, just man up to it."

"Really? And what the devil gave you that idea?" He crossed his arms over his chest.

"I say it, Doctor," she uttered, composed again. She raised her stubborn chin to him haughtily, her eyebrows knitted in a scowl.

"Stop calling me doctor, before I lose my patience with you. What the hell is going on, Erin? Did you barge in here to utter this nonsense to me? My sister is already suspicious; you have confirmed her suspicions now, you foolish girl. I'll never hear the end of it. She'll tease me until the cows come home," he scoffed in exasperation.

"Is that all you are care about, you selfish oaf? You should've told me you only wanted a good fuck. I would have done it, anyway. Hell, I needed one, too, you know!" She paused, and he raised a sculpted brow to her. "You should have said that's all it was for you. I'm a big girl; I can take it." She spoke calmly now, but she felt anything but calm.

He muttered several oaths under his breath, and she knew he was getting more vexed by his thunderous expression. "Rubbish! And you know it. Stop talking, before I get really cross with you. You are behaving like a child. I won't have this, Erin. I'm a busy man, and this is nonsense. I already explained to you."

"You are lying, because you are gutless, and you can't tell me I meant nothing to you other than a fuck. Well, assuming I was a good fuck. Who knows? I might not even be that for you, you spineless brute."

"Erin!" he bellowed.

"What? Don't like to hear the truth, do you?" She was defiant.

"You are having a tantrum. I've had enough of your silliness. You are not listening to me. I can't talk to you when you are like this," he scoffed and stepped to his desk. He rummaged in it until he picked up something out of his drawer, a smooth, flat-surfaced wooden paddle. He went to her, took her by the elbow and dragged her to his desk.

Now, bend over," he said sharply, as she looked at him with wide eyes.

"What?"

"Bend over, I said," he repeated with a small, devilish grin, as he closed the heavy drapes over the French doors to the garden.

"Marcus…"

"Erin," he repeated with an even tone, and he smacked his own hand with the paddle twice.

Her breath hitched, and her pussy tightened. She relished it somewhat, but she was dreading it too. At least he would give her his undivided attention, paddle or not. "You are n-not using t-that are you?" she stammered.

"What does it look like to you?"

"I-I…"

"I have been writing all day. My hands are tired, but you need a good paddling tonight after this childish tantrum of yours. Not to mention you already banked one in Oxford. It is about time we sort this out and remind you of the rules. Bend over and don't let me tell you again."

She rattled her head as if to say no, and his brow rose again.

"Are you refusing?" His eyes went so dark, she gulped.

"Well, I…"

"Now!" he said. His voice had a cold and commanding ring to it, but it was calm and steady. It caused her chills.

When she shook her head, not sure of this, he pounded the wooden object on the desk with a thunderous expression. It made her jump, but she jerked into motion. Erin bent over his counter. He lifted her skirt and lowered her panties, letting them fall to the floor.

"Step out of your panties," he whispered in her ear, and she did. She swallowed hard.

He used his foot to separate her legs, opening them wider.

She gasped and gave out a tiny cry, somewhere between one of excitement and dread. The cool evening air brushed against her exposed sex and skin, the titillating air fanning her clit. She complained against her predicament, lashing out a curse at him. But if she were to be honest, she was relishing the moment, though too embarrassed to admit it to herself.

He ignored her insult. He held her in position with a hand on her back. She tried to run, suddenly thinking she was not quite ready for this, but it was too late, and he pressed her down harder.

"Do not fight me. Stay still," he warned coolly.

"Marcus…" she whimpered, half wishing the paddling and half dreading it. Her pussy did a tightening exercise in anticipation. Her folds were damp from wishing it, but her brain feared it. She shot to move. But there was nowhere to go. He kept her in place.

"First, you are out of order barging into my office with no good reason other than to talk nonsense. Never do that again unless I give you permission. You have no right to interrupt me when I am working. Is that clear?" Two forceful cracks pounded her plump, creamy backside.

She shrieked. The pain took her by surprise; it was instant and excruciating compared to when he spanked her with his hand. "Marcus, please!" she begged as tears formed in her eyes. She braced her hands on the desk firmly. Her knuckles turned white as she grabbed something on it so hard. She gasped when she heard the *whoosh* of the paddle about to land on her again.

"Quiet! I have explained the reasons we must act like this." And two heavy swats struck her pert bottom.

She sobbed as she begged him to stop. "Marcus, please," she implored.

"Second, what's all this nonsense about a dirty weekend? You know I love you!" He whacked her with the wooden implement once more over each buttock.

She caught her breath, first because of the painful paddling and second at his words. He'd uttered the three famous words to her, and she had no time to enjoy them as a set of *whacks* descended on her backside. But she had heard them distinctly, and her heart leaped.

"Then, what was that? Oh, yes, oaf? Fuck? Spineless brute? You are too disrespectful! I don't want to hear you talking that way again. No insults. Understood?" he said, with two more strokes of the paddle flattening her naughty posterior.

She wriggled and squirmed, the heat in her ass flaming, but her heart and soul doing somersaults of joy at his three words. He loved her! But the paddle bounced on her backside again, taking all coherent thoughts away.

Her bottom had hurt when he spanked her with his hand after Mollie's party. But now, with the paddle... Who would have thought a small, inoffensive looking object would cause her backside to burn as if she were in an inferno. The pain was scorching, and her butt radiated with glowing redness. But his three magic words had made her resilient and happy, and she would take it anytime. Her backside stung, and she was in tears, though her wet channel was on alert, fully aroused.

Two more forceful plops of the paddle, and her pussy was launching signals to her brain that she craved to play too, and it throbbed. Oh... how the drenched slit between her legs had awakened. It was clenching. It needed action. It was telling her how much she was enjoying this, despite the burning. It dribbled. If she had to be honest, he was giving her the much-needed attention she had desired for the last two weeks.

Her self-control around this man was flimsy, and what he was doing to her turned her on, aroused her. If truth be told, she couldn't care less; she would take it anytime.

She whimpered his name, "Please, Marcus." But another set roasted her behind.

Then, he stopped. Marcus placed the paddle on his desk but didn't release his hand on her back. He pressed her there when she tried to move. "Don't," he said as he rubbed her backside and bent over, giving her light little kisses on her neck and back.

She moaned loudly when his lips brushed her skin.

"Shush, you don't wish the whole clinic to hear you, do you?" He caressed the crack of her butt as he slid his fingers to the entrance of her pussy.

"So, Miss Blake… Despite all your complaints tonight, I can see you still want me. What is it you need to tell me! Hey?"

"I-I…" she whimpered, and he walloped her backside hard with his hand.

"And don't lie."

"I want you…"

"Good, because I want you, but never have a tantrum like that again, do I make myself clear? If you need to speak to me, come and tell me without any of these dramatics, understood?"

"Yes! I am sorry," she simpered, and she tried to move, but he pressed her down on the desk with his hand.

She heard him unzip his trousers, and before she knew it, he plunged his cock inside her pussy. She moaned with joy so loud, he had to put a hand over her mouth to muffle the sound. As he pumped hard with every thrust, he crashed on her raw and tender derrière, too, sending her into a delirium of pain and pleasure mingled.

"Shush, Erin, I said. Quiet! You don't wish for everyone to hear you," he muttered through ragged breaths. He placed his hand on her clit and rubbed it while, with the other, he pinched her breast, teasing the pink buds.

His shaft pulsated inside her, and his strokes were long and forceful. Her pussy, needy and desperate for fulfilment, was engorged. So, it was not long before she shut her eyes, mumbling his name on her way to ecstasy.

He followed suit soon after and crashed on her back, satiated. They stayed like that for a few moments until he withdrew from her. He zipped himself in and lifted her from the counter, spinning her towards him. Marcus sat her on the desk, and she whimpered, as her backside was still on fire.

He smiled. "Not quite a lesson to you, is it? You like being spanked and I'm too indulgent. I'm just humouring you. But I hope you'll remember this, darling, hey?" His eyes were tender on her.

He caressed her hair, searching into her eyes. He dried the lingering tears. Marcus kissed her forehead and then her mouth, reverently, whispering little endearments as he went about kissing her all over her face.

"Oh, I missed you," she said, putting her arms around his neck, and they held each other close.

"You silly poppet! See, you are calmer now. You won't do this again, will you? Behave, my love. You know how I feel about you. Hey?" he mumbled in between kisses over her neck.

"Yes."

"Promise?"

"Yes."

They made love on the couch in his office, one more time, before he walked her back to her room, but not before he exerted another promise from her to act as agreed.

Chapter 10

Two more weeks had passed since their lovemaking evening in his office, but she stuck to her promise and kept her distance from him. For the sake of his reputation, like he had asked.

Erin wanted to please him. She realised she would have promised all, done anything, for him. If this made him happy, so be it. Besides, it was only going to be for a short while. It wasn't as if it was forever. At some point, she would leave the clinic and lead a normal life with him. So, she could behave less childish and be more grown up about his wishes as they waited for that moment. She put her soul at peace with this notion, and since she was bursting with joy, she couldn't stop her giddiness. It was as if she were a teenager; she was on cloud nine. He had said the famous three words to her. He loved her! She was delirious. That's all she craved to hear. All she cared about, and she desired nothing more.

Dr. Devlin talked about her release from the clinic, too, perhaps within a month. It meant only a few weeks, and she would be with Marcus. She hoped, forever. She sensed she was ready to go back to a normal environment, to resume living on the outside, as it should be. Her life had been on hold too long. She yearned to live and to love, with him at the centre of her universe. Leaving the clinic meant she would be free to be with him. So, things were on the up. She was full of zest.

Erin was happier than she had been in years. Even if Marcus still kept his distance from her, for appearances' sake. It wouldn't be long now until they sang their love to the world.

One morning, after Erin's session ended, Dr. Devlin asked her a few questions on the matter with Dr. Stewart, when she had barged in into his office that night.

"Please, Doctor, don't ask me. When the time comes..." She was cautious. She promised Marcus, and she would keep her pledge. But she burned red. She suspected that his sister was aware of what was going on, more than anyone imagined.

The young woman smiled but accepted Erin's silence. "I won't press you on this, but when you are ready, you will tell me everything. That brother of mine can be a bit of a bear sometimes. I hope for some good news soon," Dr. Devlin said with amusement in her eyes and a wink, while her patient blushed furiously.

Erin thought Dr. Devlin knew what was going on between them, though she feigned ignorance. Perhaps she was not the only one. It seemed to her as if it was only to please Marcus that everyone pretended not to know.

"Thank you, Doctor."

"Here, would you mind taking these invoices to Marcus for me? He needs to sign them."

"Yes, of course, Doctor," she agreed with eagerness. She thanked her for the session, grabbed the papers and left.

Erin made her way to the other side of the building, to the waiting room of Dr. Stewart's office. Nurse Stevenson wasn't at her desk, and the door to Marcus's office was shut. She didn't know what to do. If the door was closed, it indicated he had someone with him or he wasn't to be disturbed. She put her ear to it, like she usually did, and could hear talking inside.

He had given her butt a good thrashing with the paddle for interrupting him last time. The thought made her pussy clench. A bolt shot straight to it at the recollection. Who would have believed she enjoyed having her bottom spanked and paddled? *Wow!* It was news to her. Her folds dampened of their own volition, thinking of his firm hand on her buttocks.

Blast! But for now, she had to wait. Her backside had been tender for two days after that, so she decided against interrupting him. She plopped the invoices on the nurse's desk and wrote her a note to deliver them to Dr. Stewart.

Erin was about to leave, but that meant she wouldn't see him, and she was desperate for a glimpse of him, even for a moment. So, she decided to give him the papers in person but left them on the nurse's desk with the note as they were, in case whoever was in there was going to be too long. She sat in an armchair to bide her time. She thought it would not harm her to wait for a few minutes. She might be lucky, and Marcus would finish his meeting soon...

A noise made her jump. The door to his office had become unlatched. Maybe when she leaned on it, she had pushed it open by mistake? Perhaps! She could hear the voices now with the door ajar.

Curiosity got the better of her. She got up and tiptoed to the door. She held her breath. One false movement, and they would discover her. Oh, she could not bear the humiliation if she was caught. He would think she was spying on him. So, she was careful not to make a sound.

She peered through the tiny crack of the door inside his office. It was then her heart sunk! She saw them. Erin wanted the earth to swallow her. She wanted to die.

Marcus had his arm around the nurse's shoulder with a loving smile on his face, and then he kissed the top of Stevenson's pretty blonde hair. For someone so stern and so upright about his reputation, it was a too familiar gesture with a member of staff. From both of them!

The nurse rested her head on Marcus's chest and covered his hand on her shoulder with hers.

Erin's breathing stopped. The room twirled around her. She thought she was going to faint, so she took deep breaths to calm herself. She withdrew, silently. Erin had seen enough. It horrified her. Her heart ached in agony!

Her head in turmoil, she pressed a hand hard over her mouth, to stop herself from whimpering, and the other on the wall, to steady herself from the dizzy spell. When she recovered sufficiently, she willed herself to the nurse's desk, trying to conceal herself. The note she had written was still on the papers. She tiptoed out of the room in disgust.

Now, she needed that distance from him, as far away from him as she could go. For once, she was glad for that distance. The penny had dropped. She ran through the long hallway to her bedroom, not even seeing where she was going, with tears blurring her vision.

This was the reason he wanted it like this and had pushed her to be silent about their relationship. *The bastard! Reputation, my ass! Even the clinic's reputation was a lie.* Nurse Stevenson was the real reason for his secrecy. *The blackguard! The beast, the swine!*

She was hurt, devastated, and humiliated! She became infuriated, so much so, she would have slapped the damn man repeatedly if she'd had the chance.

Erin paced her bedroom as if she were a caged animal, blabbering improprieties at him. He'd deceived her. Marcus had lied to her. He just wanted to keep her quiet while at the clinic. It was all a horrible lie. She trotted back and forth in her square room like a frantic lioness ready for the kill. Not even when Goran and Lily came knocking at her door to check on her, could it release her from her agony.

She feigned a headache to be left alone. Then, she launched herself on her bed and cried herself to sleep, heartbroken.

Chapter 11

She recalled her first day at the clinic, her initial session with Dr. Devlin.

Her session with the competent doctor mellowed her and changed her mind. She had never believed in this kind of therapy. But Erin had soon seen the value of it in that one session. It helped to talk to her, to share her burden.

At first, she had lain on the couch, saying nothing. Not a word left her lips while staring at the ceiling, embarrassed, answering in monosyllables the questions the doctor asked. She was uneasy. Though Erin soon relaxed and opened up to her slowly. By the end of that initial meeting, she was blabbering, sometimes incoherently. She talked about everything that came into her mind.

Sitting on Dr. Devlin's couch, she babbled on about the death of her twin brother, Professor Peter Blake, about the horrendous three, desperate, long days she waited for her twin's return from Antibes. The crushing feeling when she realised he would not return. She cried for a while without a word. Dr. Devlin never pushed her.

Erin talked about her guilt at being alive while her twin was dead. Losing her brother, even if her twin had been anything but a model of endeavours, it felt to her as if she had lost a limb. She had been bereft, her sadness exacerbated by the death of her parents soon after, and in quick succession.

Her entire family had gone in such a brief space of time, and it devastated her, plunging her into a depression, a living hell. They had left her in a rotten world to cope with it all alone.

She talked about the void in her heart that was overpowering her, squeezing her out of her sanity. Erin talked for hours. She started uncertainly, timid, but then the words gushed out of her mouth like a waterfall cascading over the edge of a cliff. An unstoppable torrent of words, not always lucid, not always clear, but it began to set her free.

She talked until her time was up, nonstop, and it felt cleansing, liberating her somewhat from her anguish. The feelings she'd bottled up for almost a year came out in words, firing out of her lips like bullets at a shooting range.

Dr. Devlin listened. She commented at the appropriate moment. She told Erin those feelings were natural, not to be ashamed of them. Above all, the doctor told her not to blame herself for any of it, that her twin's death was not her fault. She asked the proper questions. She encouraged her, homing in during some difficult moments to aid the understanding of her feelings. So, the two hours passed as if they were a minute.

Strangely, for the first time in almost a year, Erin had a lightness of heart, a brightness in her soul. Just a touch, not much, but it was there, palpable enough for her to look forward to seeing the doctor again the next day.

After months of darkness, of living in the twilight, for once, Erin felt positive. She saw a sliver of light beckoning her.

An exceptional psychiatrist, Dr. Devlin, helped her to get better over the months, and she had appreciated her assistance. She owed the young doctor her sanity, which, in her darkest hours, she saw slipping away from her as she contemplated ending it all.

Erin was grateful to her for bringing her out of the darkness, for restoring her to life. She would leave the clinic in a few weeks, healed. Or as much as anyone like her could be healed.

But the scene Erin had witnessed between Marcus and Nurse Stevenson had plunged her back into her agony, into her torture, a unique type of misery, a different type of torture. This one was of the heart, about love. But the agony was just as strong and debilitating.

She felt like a freakish ghost ambling aimlessly through life again.

So, the next day, she remained in her bedroom, feigning a headache. She wished to see nobody. She paced the room for hours, with in-between spells of violent weeping about him. Erin was going out of her mind with grief. She would die of a broken heart, the pain in her soul was so harrowing. That was until rage took over. A fury so strong, so overpowering, she figured she could bat Marcus on the head. She was so angry with him, she could slap his face until she got that annoying grin out of his lips. She launched a myriad of expletives towards him for lying to her. *The hypocrite! The bastard!*

Erin whipped herself into a frenzy of frustration. If she didn't do something, she would go insane. Oh, but she would not give Marcus the satisfaction of letting him see her like this. Downtrodden, no! *The monster!*

She reached for the window, opening it to take a bit of fresh air. She inhaled in big gulps, and she stared at the garden as tears poured down her cheeks.

Suddenly, she saw Dr. Bell, the new doctor. He was arriving for his night shift. The new doctor had created quite a stir amongst the female population of the clinic with his good looks and charming manner. Every time he was around, all the girls batted their eyelashes and giggled foolishly at everything he said.

An idea came into her head. She would give the hideous monster a bit of his own medicine. She turned to her wardrobe and searched for it. And there it was.

Half an hour on, Erin entered the dining area. But, oh boy, it was a grand entrance. People gathering for dinner stared at her agape when she showed up. It stunned the room into silence as she walked in. The red, short, hot little dress she had worn at Mollie's party wrapped around her frame like a glove. She looked stunning. Her amazing legs seemed longer than ever under the short frock, and her enticing, prosperous half round globes of creamy skin that were her bosom, spilled out the plunging neckline.

It shocked everyone.

Her long hair cascaded, luscious at the back, rather than in her usual ponytail. She had put on lipstick, and as a makeup artist, she had done a grand job on herself. Her lips were as red and alluring as the dress, her makeup flawless, something she had refused to do at Mollie's party.

That night in the bastard's precious clinic, she had every intention to show him the real siren she had so frightfully tried to dampen at the party.

As Erin made her way to her friends' table, from the corner of her eyes, she didn't miss Marcus's jaw drop. With his warning never to wear that dress again still ringing in her ear, it felt sinfully satisfying to provoke him.

The blackguard!

"Good God, I say. Wow!" Goran gawked at her, and he whistled until Lily slapped his arm. "What? I'm just saying!"

"Darling, you look fit to kill in that red-hot number," Belinda said with a naughty smile, "My question is who do you intend to hit tonight like this?"

Erin sat at the table with a blush.

"I'll say. I will have to steal that frock from you for my next movie. Every man in the room is ogling you. Our Goran here, too." It put Lily out, and she darted a scowl at him.

"Oh, but you missed Dr. Stewart's expression. See his face? He is thundering. What a dress! Even Bell has your full attention." Belinda winked at her.

Erin turned towards Dr. Bell, and she gave him a languid, sinful, slow smile and waved at him. The young doctor's expression danced with delight.

Seconds later, Marcus stood and went out of the room. His eyes scorched her with lust and rebuke as he stepped out. If she had to guess, it was disapproval she saw in his eyes.

How dare he? The brute!

Thus, suddenly, Erin felt foolish and way too self-conscious in the silly dress, out of place in the clinic. Perhaps this had not been one of her finest ideas.

She went to the buffet to get some food. Everyone was still staring at her, and it made her feel evil. Besides, it was no fun. The man himself was not in the room anymore. She tried to eat a bit, but she couldn't. Her stomach and throat closed up on her.

The result, she felt worse than before. She excused herself after a while, saying her headache had returned with a vengeance. She went back to her room, feeling humiliated. The difference, this time, the humiliation had been her own doing. So, she wept at her stupidity, at her foolishness, but mostly, she cried her eyes out for him.

This crazy idea had been his fault, though. *He betrayed me! How dare he look at me so affronted? The liar! The beast! He took advantage of me. How could he? What a monster!*

She had meant nothing to him. She'd been just a fuck for him; she realised it now. Erin had been right all along. She had been a dirty weekend for him. Erin had known it all along but had dismissed the truth. She had wanted to believe in him. But she should have known better. It was all an illusion.

The look on his face when he touched the young nurse's shoulders… it pained her.

Suddenly, her chest felt constricted. She couldn't breathe. Her face was puffy and red from too much crying. She kept sniffing and wiping her nose, and she emptied an entire box of tissues. She didn't stop weeping until she fell asleep, exhausted, in the early hours of the morning.

That next day, she sat on her bed, still in her pajamas, even if it was midday. Goran had brought a breakfast tray to her, but it was sitting on the desk untouched. She couldn't eat a morsel.

How would she face Marcus again after last night, knowing what she knew about him and the nurse?

She rubbed her chest with her palm as if she wanted to lessen the suffering in her heart. The pain was there, and no amount of rubbing would take that away. It hurt like hell.

She had been a game for him. All the while, he loved the young nurse. He was a liar and a cheat. Shame on him!

One thing was weird, though, as she sat there on her bed, mourning her lost love, and sending blasphemous curses to Marcus. Snippets of her dream came to mind. She dreamt of the regatta.

Erin hadn't attended the Henley's Regatta in years or been anywhere near the river for ages. In her dream, she was happy and bouncing around on the riverbank in a pretty dress with not a care in the world. At one point, Marcus appeared.

She said his name several times, calling out to him. He sat by the river with her, smiling at her. But then she awakened with a start when he scowled at her. He vanished as she opened her eyes to a new, sad day, full of agony, knowing that he didn't want her. Was it wishful thinking on her part? It seemed strange to her to fantasise about the regatta; she hadn't thought of it for so long. In particular, to conceive a happy dream in her present agony was preposterous. She couldn't make heads or tails of it. So, she dismissed the silly notion.

Go figure out my twisted mind! Perhaps it's a way to cope with the pain in my heart, telling me something. It's time to call it a day. That was it, she convinced herself. The dream told her to move on, to go away. *Leave him; he doesn't want you.* Besides, she couldn't risk humiliating herself again because of him.

She locked herself in her room, not wanting to see anybody. She had seen her friends, but she wished to be alone. Erin feigned she had caught the flu, thus accounting for her puffy, blotchy face, red eyes, and runny nose from all that crying.

One thing was certain, she would not stay at the clinic any longer, even if her release was imminent and within a few weeks. She would have to get away. She couldn't wait, and the sooner, the better.

Chapter 12

Two days later, Erin was writing her letters. She addressed one to Zac, thanking him for taking care of her expenses at the clinic through the months, and for being so forgiving with her, despite the troublesome past with her twin brother.

Her second letter was to Finley. She thanked him for his understanding and sending her to the clinic rather than to prison for stalking and scaring Kathryn in her moments of madness.

She was glad she resolved her differences with Mollie and Kathryn. It was all forgiven, and the past forgotten on both sides; only new beginnings counted.

Rather than to write to the girls, she would tell them herself when the time came. When the fuss had died down, she would explain. She valued her friendship with them.

She wrote to Goran, to ask for forgiveness for what she was about to do. No doubt they would blame him for it. *That's why he mustn't know of my plan. He must suspect nothing.*

Her last letter was to Dr. Stewart. They were difficult letters to compose.

She ignored Goran's knocks on her door. She wished to be left alone, and she didn't let him in. Erin feigned a foul mood on top of a terrible flu. She avoided everyone for two days, pretending to be ill.

"We can have a dinner tray in your room if you feel up to it, with Dr. Devlin's approval," he said through the door, and she agreed. At least, he would leave her alone until then. She needed time to think.

The letter to Marcus was the most difficult one to write. She found the words easier on her seventh attempt. She poured her soul out, her love for him, in black and white. She understood why they wouldn't be together. His heart belonged to someone else. She forgave him, too, she wrote. She would never regret the time she spent with him but would cherish the memory instead, despite everything. Erin cared for him too much to hate him for long. So, she finished her letter amongst weeping and wailing for him.

She resolved she would leave the clinic. She couldn't bear it, being so near to Marcus and yet so far. It hurt her to know he loved another, and now, it was she who wished to have the distance between them.

She would get over him. It would be hard, but she had to. Though, if she had to be honest, she had cried for days since she saw him with Nurse Stevenson. Her position in the clinic was hopeless, absurd, under the circumstances. Not to mention the sinful embarrassment of the red dress. *God, what possessed her to do that?*

Everything had turned into a shambles, impossible now. She had to run. Even if it was a few weeks before her official release from the place, she wouldn't stay another day. She couldn't bear it. She had to go.

She hadn't spoken to Marcus about what she had seen in his office. She wouldn't give him the satisfaction of seeing her so upset. That, she wouldn't do. Besides, he must suspect nothing before she left the clinic. Or he might concoct some other lie to keep her.

No. She would go without telling him anything, without telling him she knew about his affair with Stevenson. Her letter would tell him, anyway, after she'd left.

Erin had to complete a plan to leave the clinic tonight, without raising the alarm, and without Goran noticing her escape. That would be tricky. She took a hanky from her pocket to dry her tears.

She saw the sleeping pills Dr. Devlin gave her when she had gone through a period when she could not sleep. In the end, she had not taken them, but they would come in handy for her plan now.

Erin knew what to do.

DINNER TIME CAME. On cue, Goran, Belinda and Lily called upon her with a trolly full of trays.

"Why are they letting you stay in my room for supper tonight? They are not so forthcoming like this," she asked, cautiously referring to the strict rules of the clinic.

"Well, I have my convincing ways, you know," Goran dismissed her question, and the girls agreed. He drew her attention to the food instead, knowing she hadn't eaten much lately.

"The doctors are worried about you, and they sent us to cheer you up. But you must eat," Belinda said with anxiety. She couldn't conceal her concern for her friend.

Erin had hidden her letters; she would leave them in Dr. Stewart's office later. She packed her stuff, too. She left out only things on show, so as not to raise any suspicion from her companions. She would be ready to go when everyone went to sleep. She would miss them. She had grown attached to them.

That night, her friends were excellent company, more than usual, and she would have enjoyed the early evening meal were it not for the fact she would have to drug Goran in order to make her escape.

The girls' rooms were at the back of the building, so no one would notice her missing until the morning. Goran's room was next door to hers. He was the bodyguard Finley had assigned to her all those months ago, at the outset, when her grief had been at her most perverse, making her do awful things to Kathryn. So, Goran was there to make sure she did no mischief and followed through with her therapy at the clinic with no misbehaviour, to guard her from herself, so to speak.

A friendship had grown between them over the months. Lately, he was her bodyguard in name only since they trusted each other. A trust she would break tonight, but she had no choice. He would raise the alarm if he knew. So, she would have to deal with him, even if she felt sorry and vile about doing it.

He kept her spirits up during dinner, telling her funny stories of when he was in the army. He joined at twenty-one and posted abroad on army errands. He was entertaining them with his tales. He only told them those humorous ones, not the doom and gloom of being a soldier in a foreign, dangerous land, with death often on his doorstep.

The evening passed joyously, although Erin was on alert. She never lost sight of her aim that night, of what she was required to do when the time came. She desired to set her plan in motion. She would leave the clinic tonight, in secret.

So, at the end of the meal, she offered to make tea. Unbeknown to her friend, she crushed the sleeping pills into Goran's cup, ensuring he drank it all. He started yawning after a while from the effects of the pills. But she needed to have him and the girls out of her room to get things moving.

"Sorry to be a spoilsport. I am exhausted today and still under the weather with this damn flu. You don't mind if I go to bed, do you?" she faked to get them out.

"You are a mood breaker, darling," Lily said, "but I am bushed. I need my bed, too."

"I'll be in the reading room for a while if you need me," Goran added, when he was on the threshold.

Erin stopped him for a second by grabbing his elbow. "You are a nice man, Goran, you know. The girl who lands you will be a lucky woman," Erin said and then smiled at Lily, who blushed, while Belinda winked, teasing her.

"Well, thank you!" he replied, lifting his eyebrows. "I have to find the lady first since no one will have me," he answered with mirth in his eyes, and he kissed her cheek.

Then he looked at her pensively. "Are you sure it's just the flu?"

"Yes, this damn flu is getting the better of me. I just want to go to bed." She sniffed all the more to make a show of it.

"Okay, as you wish."

"Good night."

Her friends took the trolly with the trays and left.

She gave a sigh of relief. The girls were going to bed and Goran would soon fall asleep, she hoped... Erin had crushed three pills in his cup of tea. The instructions said one-a-night or two. But she needed to make sure he went to sleep fast and as deep as a hibernating bear, so, she gave him three. The reading room was excellent for her purpose. People didn't go in there too often in the evening, so no one would disturb him.

A tick in the box for the first part of her plan. She would look in on him later to ensure he was asleep and that the girls were safely out of her way in their rooms. Then, she would go to the unmanned surveillance room. The idea was to turn off the cameras of the surveillance system then open the electric gates to the estate from that room, for her to make her escape.

On one occasion, the security cameras crashed. Goran had gone to the surveillance room to fix them. The system came from Zac's security firm. She'd gone with him and watched Goran work on them, turning them on and off. It wouldn't be too taxing for her.

She would borrow his car to leave the clinic. That, perhaps, might be a little trickier since she needed to find the keys. She would send a letter to him, telling him where he would recover it again—no text messages, or they could trace her.

That night, time passed slowly. She was troubled by doing all these underhanded things to her friends, but she had no choice. She must go, and she knew no other way. But when her thoughts went to Marcus with Nurse Stevenson, a pang of pain shot through her body, and she wished to die. Her situation was impossible. She could not bear to see him around. It hurt her too much.

She had said nothing to Marcus about her discovery. She wouldn't give him the satisfaction to see her crying and upset. Oh, no, she wouldn't tolerate it. He would lie and deny it. So why bother? She knew the score when men lied about these things. She had been there before, her ex-fiancé had been a master of deceit. Erin would not go there with Marcus. She would not allow it. So, she kept her discovery to herself; she told no one. Marcus would read her letter, anyway...

He didn't want her in his life; he wanted the nurse. That was obvious to her. But he could not avoid her in the clinic. So, she would make it easier for him and disappear. She would go tonight, and it wouldn't be too soon...

Erin finished her packing. Opening the closet, she came upon a bottle of wine she had purchased long ago when she first arrived at the clinic, on the first night. Alcohol was a no-no there. Marcus had strictly forbidden it. So, she kept it under wraps, hidden at the bottom of her wardrobe, tucked away for a special occasion. The nurse hadn't found this bottle when she'd confiscated the rest on that first night. She had concealed it for months from everybody. She had even forgotten about it. That night, waiting for Goran to fall asleep, made her feel anxious. She felt distressed about her plan, too. So, she fished out the bottle. In the absence of a corkscrew, Erin pushed the cork forcefully into the bottle. It took her a little time and strength, but she managed it. She had learned nothing in her long years at boarding school, but it had equipped her with tiny, useful, whimsical skills like this one.

She felt awful for Goran; he had only shown her kindness, but it couldn't be helped. So, while she waited for him to fall asleep, she drained the water out and filled the glass with wine instead. She drank it in one go. *God, I needed that drink!* she thought with a sigh of relief. She poured herself another glass and gulped it.

"Steady, you don't want to get drunk tonight of all nights, when you need your wits about you," she murmured to herself.

She looked in on Goran. She peeked through the crack of the door ajar in the room, saw him yawning, but he was still awake, reading.

Damn!

The girls were not there, so she assumed they had gone to bed. Thank God for small mercies.

She returned to her room. Perhaps, she had not put enough sleeping pills in his drink... What now? She would wait fifteen minutes more and check on him again. She was sure he drank all his tea. Erin went back to check on him later. Peeking at Goran through the door again, she saw the book on the floor and his head on his chest. He was asleep.

She stepped in and called out his name, but he was out cold. Faint noises emanated from his mouth, she assumed were snores. *Success at last!*

She returned to her room, and in her distress, she poured herself another cup of wine for the road. Her hands were shaking, and she was trembling all over. She wasn't sure if it was the thrill of the escape, the vile underhandedness at her lies to her friends, or the massive pain in her heart and soul at never seeing Marcus again.

She dismissed the turmoil in her thoughts and focused on her plan. She gulped down the rest of the liquid in her glass to calm herself. She took deep breaths.

Erin planned to drive to the village in Goran's car then leave his car at the station. She would catch a late train going to Oxford. She would change there and go on to London, hoping they would lose her tracks from there. She would hide somewhere in London until things calmed down. It was the last train of the day. If she missed it, she would be in trouble. The trip to the village would take her roughly twenty-five minutes, perhaps less at night. She would do all of this in the pitch dark of the countryside, in the dead of night.

Erin looked at the clock and it was already nine-fifteen. Lights went out by ten pm in the clinic. She had to hurry. She made her way next door, to Goran's room, to get the keys to his car. She got in and went to his desk. She searched, but the keys weren't there. She checked in the drawers and in his jackets, but they weren't there, either. Ten minutes later, she had looked everywhere. There were few hiding places in a small room.

Silly me, I should have found out beforehand where he kept his keys. Or maybe they are on him... Oh, no, she would have to go through him. She walked back to her room to calm herself for a minute. Yes, she couldn't avoid it; she would have to search him.

Oh, Lord!

She poured herself another glass of wine, she was so distraught. Erin had to find the keys; she had no back-up plan. She gulped half of the wine, trying to calm her nerves.

She went to the reading room. It was still empty. She called out his name, just in case. "Goran?" she said twice, but he was out, fast asleep. She searched his trouser pockets, front and back, as delicately as she could. It was soon obvious the keys to his car were not on him, either.

Stupid girl! They are in the car!

She returned to her room to get the letters, made her way to Dr. Stewart's office, hoping he was not working late. She was lucky; he had gone for the night. She left them concealed in a drawer in his desk. Then, hastily, she went back to her room to pick up her stuff and be gone.

In the dead of night, she crossed the extensive grounds towards Goran's car, near the cottages, parked on the other side of the estate. She dragged her bags across with her.

There were two cottages on the grounds. They were about fifty meters in, either side of the electronic gates' entrance to the estate. One, a large cottage on the left, semi-hidden by high hedges, the other lay on the right of the gates. The large cottage belonged to Dr. Stewart while the other to his sister, Dr. Devlin.

After a few generous glasses of wine, Erin realised she was a little tipsy despite looking fine on the surface. In her slightly inebriated state, her manner became quite lax. She scolded herself, getting annoyed. It was easy to commit errors of judgement if she was not careful, she told herself.

Focus, Erin, focus! Stop fooling around!

HE'D BEEN in an atrocious mood for two days after seeing Erin in that red dress at dinner. When she entered the dining room in that frock, Marcus almost had a coronary. God! He couldn't deny she looked hot and sexy. Though for her to parade herself, in his clinic of all places, in such a manner, had sent him into a spiralling fury.

He had to master all his self-control not to jump on his feet, grab her arm, and drag her out of there. He would have spanked the daylights out of her, make no mistake, if he had. She would not have sat pretty for days, the frivolous minx. Under the circumstances, he had done the best he could; he left the room, directing at her a glance mingled with fire and ice. If she had not been so upset with him, it would have told her better than to embark on that plan of hers.

The next day, worry replaced his awful temper when his sister informed him Erin had the flu and taken to her bed. That night, he decided he would look in on her in the morning, to make sure she was okay and have a little chat about the dress. No doubt the silly little dress contributed to making herself ill; there was nothing to it. He'd roast her ass when the time came for wearing that damn thing again. He swore he would burn the evil frock when he got his hands on it.

"Come and have a look at this." His sister's voice took him out of his reverie.

"What is it?" he replied from the sitting room in his cottage.

Marcus was finally relaxing after a long day. He didn't wish to rise from his comfy armchair by the fire on a chilly night. He relished a tête-à-tête with his book and a brandy.

That evening, Marcus and his sister had finished a lengthy session in his cottage on medical issues. They had preferred the relaxed atmosphere of his sitting room at home rather than his office at the clinic. It was way past office hours. They opted for this, as it involved only the two of them.

Julia had just stepped into his study at the cottage, to deposit on his desk the stack of papers they'd reviewed, before leaving for the night.

"Marcus, bloody hell. Come here, I tell you, now. Move it!" his sister cried out. By the urgency in her tone, he realised something was amiss.

He joined her. "What is it?" he repeated from the doorway. He exhaled in a huff. He was none too pleased to be disturbed.

"Look at this," she urged, pointing at the monitor on his desk. "Miss Blake is in Goran's car. She is trying to find something, not sure what she's doing, but she seems a bit... well, unsteady on her feet."

In her state of inebriation and anxiety, Erin had committed her first error, a rather fundamental one. She had forgotten to turn off the security cameras and the control system on the estate.

"For Heaven's sake! She's drunk!" Marcus blurted as his jaw dropped. He saw Erin through the monitor of the surveillance system on his desk. "Bloody hell, what's wrong with the minx?"

She was coming out of the driving seat of Goran's car, stumbling in the dark, almost falling and getting up again, unsteady on her feet. She made her way to the passenger door.

"Umm... What are we going to do?" his sister asked him with her eyes glued to the monitor, watching her.

"Where the hell is Goran?" Marcus urged. "Isn't he supposed to be her bodyguard? Why is he allowing this? Who caused her to drink?"

"I don't know. He is not with her."

"Call the night nurse. Ask her to tell Goran to come and pick Erin up immediately! God, there is no end to the nonsense of this woman. Watch her until he comes."

"Me?"

"She is your patient, Julia. You said so yourself, and I am finished for the day, trust me. What the devil is she looking for, I wonder?" he replied with a small grin, despite his annoyance, and shook his head in resignation with a sigh. "She'll only antagonise me in that state if I go out there. Besides, if I get my hands on her, drunk and all, I won't be responsible if I give her ass another good thrashing. She needs a spanking for this little charade, and I am too tired for this tonight. I'll speak to her tomorrow." The word 'speak' had another meaning in his mind, and it envisaged his firm hand bouncing on her backside.

"You spanked her?" Julia asked him with eyes as big as the moon, mouth agape.

"Close your mouth, dear. The nurse, call her! Now. My book and brandy are waiting for me," he said with a slow grin.

"Oh, Marcus, really!" his sister exclaimed and flushed when his words hit home.

"Call matron, now," he repeated with urgency, winked at her and left the room.

"This is Dr. Devlin, could you please get Mr. Marshall and instruct him to come immediately to Dr. Stewart's cottage? Miss Blake is trying to find something in his car, but she is a little tipsy. He must pick her up at once, on the double."

"Oh, that girl can be trouble."

"Matron, tell Mr. Marshall to hurry," Julia said with a stern lilt in her voice. She was gentle, but she knew when to be bossy when the time dictated.

"Yes, Doctor, of course." It prompted the woman on the phone, and she went to do her bidding.

As Julia kept watching Erin on the monitor, if Dr. Stewart thought his night would comprise of reading a book with a glass of brandy, he was mistaken.

"Marcus, come here, quickly!" his sister screamed after a few minutes. The alarm in her tone made him jump out of his armchair and run.

"Look," Julia said, pointing at the monitor again when he was beside her. They both gawked at the screen, horrified, as they watched Erin slip into Dr. Stewart's convertible.

"She is in your car!" Julia cried out in distress.

"Yes, I can see that. What the devil is she looking for in there?" he asked in a high-pitched voice.

"How do I know? But what if she is not looking for anything, but she is trying to go somewhere?"

"Go? Go where? What do you mean?"

"Yes, Marcus! You didn't see it, but she has her bags with her," Julia said in concern in a rather petulant tone, as if he was a little slow.

"Her bags? Well, she won't go anywhere in my car," he replied with a scowl and a sigh, but when his sister blinked rapidly, agape and blanched, he knew. "Tell me you didn't leave the keys in the ignition." His eyes went wide, staring at her.

"Well, I-I… "

"Oh, bloody hell, open the damn gates, *now!* The silly woman may try to gate crash out of here," he shouted as he ran out of the room, just when the phone rang.

He was already at the front door when Julia came running after him. "Matron cannot wake Goran up; he is out cold, and Erin is trying the ignition in your car."

"Jesus!" he blurted a curse. "Go up to the clinic and see to Goran. I am going after her before she kills herself or somebody else." And he ran out of the door.

"Be careful!" his sister yelled after him.

Chapter 13

E rin's head was throbbing. The keys were not in Goran's car, either. She muttered under her breath in irritation. She would have to return to the clinic to look for the keys again. Someone might see her now. Her plan would soon be discovered if she wasn't careful, not good at all. As she passed by Dr. Stewart's car, the soft-top of his blue convertible was down, and she noticed the keys were in the ignition. It was a stroke of luck.

Oh, God, could she take the man's car? Could she possibly do it? Well, she was going to take Goran's, anyway. Did it matter which one she took... *or borrowed*... she liked that word better. No, it didn't really matter! She would be in trouble, regardless of which car she used. A devilish smile curled up on her lips. And Marcus deserved it for being a liar.

She threw her bags in the tiny backseat of his car. As she was unsteady on her feet, one of her bags landed by the passenger door on the gravel pavement instead. She mumbled a curse under her breath. She bent down to collect it, hitting her head on the side mirror of the car on her way up.

"Bloody hell!" she yelled at the sharp pain in her head. "Shush," she told herself with a finger to her nose. A rivulet of blood came down to the side of her face. She took a hanky from her pocket and dabbed it, moaning in pain and panicking somewhat. Sweet Jesus, this was not in her plan, either.

She put the bag in the backseat, then jumped into the driving seat. She started the car, the ignition on. Erin swore when she saw the gates of the estate closed. She was intoxicated, no doubt, but not to the extent to think she could crash the iron gates open with the car. She was not drunk enough to realise she had made two huge mistakes. She hadn't turned off the security cameras, nor had she opened the electronic gates to let herself out of the estate. In fact, she'd missed that step from her plan, entirely. More curses flooded her brain and tumbled out of her mouth, cursing her stupidity. As she was muttering to herself and blaming her foolishness for her run of bad luck, the gates opened as if by magic.

Whoever did it, thinks I'm the doctor. She grinned at her sudden turn of luck. She revved the car on, but she struggled with the gearstick, it wouldn't shift into first gear.

Erin's own car was an automatic. She had never driven an expensive convertible, and it was at least ten years since she had used a manual gearstick. So, there was an abrupt and jarring sound of metal coming from the gearbox, grinding and scraping as she tried to shift it. In her inebriated condition, her coordination between shifting the gearstick into position and pressing down on the clutch pedal with her foot was not happening. As she was still struggling with this, she heard someone yell.

"What the hell are you doing?" Marcus thundered from somewhere behind the car. His voice was dark with undertones, as if ready for lightning to strike.

Erin recognised his voice and the uncompromising tone, without the need to turn and glance at him. Her eyes became round and big. He had an unobstructed view of her in the driving seat, with the top of his convertible rolled down.

She mumbled another curse under her breath, and for a second, she panicked. But then the stick went into the right gear position, she stepped on the accelerator, and she was off. The car jerked forward.

Marcus cursed, seeing it move. "Stop, Erin!" he cried out after her, but it was clear she had no intention of stopping.

Marcus was a tall, fit man, about six feet and three inches. He ran five miles twice a week on the hills in the countryside. So, he went fast after her.

She had to negotiate the width of the gates—badly, he would add at that precise moment—since he saw one side of his expensive convertible scraping the iron gates with a big gash appearing on the length of it. That slowed her down for a few seconds, and it was enough for him to catch up with her alongside the vehicle.

"Stop, you foolish woman!" he howled, warning her with a thunderous expression on his face, as he kept on running in parallel with the vehicle while it left the estate and turned onto the road. When he realised she had no intention of stopping and she was getting away from him as she got used to the gearstick, he had no choice.

He dove onto the back of the car with several black curses, just about dragging himself onto it by the scrap of his neck.

For once, Marcus was glad his sister had left the top of his convertible down, even if this would normally infuriate him. In that instance, he thanked his lucky stars, or Erin would have gone away from him.

As it was, he landed on the trunk of the car, his gigantic hands gripping mighty strong the mound of the rolled down hood at the back, behind the tiny backseat. He held onto it as if for dear life, while the vehicle swayed this way and that in her panic, his elegant leather house slippers on his feet, scraping the pavement. He was sure they were about to catch fire.

"For God's sake, stop the damn car! You are going to kill us!" he roared, certain his days were about to come to a tragic end that night.

She glanced over her shoulder in terror when she heard his voice. When she saw him hanging by a thread on the trunk, she screamed. Erin slammed on the brakes hard, with all her might, and the convertible screeched to a halt. The sudden stop jerked him forward in one big motion and he flew headfirst down into the tiny backseat. He landed badly on her bags, upside down, cursing like a trooper. And a brusque pain jolted in his shoulder and ran to his brain as he hauled an unrepeatable and blasphemous imprecation.

She turned and peeked over her shoulders. She realised he was in the car seat behind her. She saw his legs and his scrumptious backside awkwardly sticking up from the back. She didn't know what to do. Erin bit her lower lip, chewing the soft flesh in agony. So, she did the only thing that occurred to her. Her foot slammed on the gas again, all the way down, at full throttle. The car jolted and boomed forward at high speed as the wheels rubbed jarringly on the pavement.

He cursed as he was tossed and jostled around against her bags, upside down. He was thrown here and there in the back like a pendulum swinging in every direction. A big a man as he was, with his bottom sticking up in the tiny backseat of his convertible advancing at this speed, his body felt like a church bell hammer, striking the sides of the car fast and furious in all directions.

"God, if you don't kill us tonight, I swear, I am going to kill you the second I land my hands on you. Stop!" Marcus was beyond furious. He was conscious, even upside down, of the vehicle veering and swerving. It went this way and that on the road.

Her driving was maniacal. No mean feat since she was intoxicated and panicking, out of control. Her erratic drive making it impossible for him to turn himself the right way up, as it whirled him back and forth and left to right in the car.

Her terror of him was multiplying.

He yelled at her a few times to stop the vehicle. But she didn't. In her panic and dread, she drove faster, with the car dangerously scraping the wall in the narrow lane outside the perimeter of the clinic. It took him about a minute, big and tall as he was, to swing himself around in the tiny backseat. He regained his balance, the right way up again. His head popped up from the back, finally upright, and he launched two of her bags out of the backseat in fury with dark imprecations he wasn't aware he knew. As he did so, the car scraped the wall until it turned onto the main road.

"Turn on the headlights, woman!" he cried out through gritted teeth with unrepeatable curses.

"Ooh, sure!"

"Stop!"

"Stop? Lights? Which is it?"

"For crying out loud, drop this nonsense, *now*."

"Where are the lights?" The car skidded on the opposite side in the upcoming traffic lane as she searched for the headlight button on the dashboard. Lucky for them, it was deserted then. She wasn't looking where she was going on the road.

His eyes wide in consternation, he was past cursing; he was so enraged, he could not find his voice. Marcus opened his mouth to say something, but nothing came out. He raised himself up from the backseat and crossed over, but not before an abrupt swerve of the car almost forced him out. Somehow, he managed to hang on. When he was steady again, he jumped and tumbled onto the passenger seat in the front. He was now sitting next to her.

She turned to him, and their eyes locked for a second. Even in the dark, she couldn't miss the fire in his eyes. They were glowing red, like those of a demon. She gulped and trembled in fear. In her panic, she drove faster.

He was seething, and for once, it pleased him that she trembled in fear at seeing him.

She would have sworn she could see smoke billowing from his head, his face a thunderous mask.

He slapped her hands on the steering-wheel, hard.

"Cut it out!"

He struggled to lose her grip on it.

"Ouch, ouch." She clutched it with all the force she possessed, as if gale winds were about to rip it off her.

The car pulled to the left and then to the right dangerously; they were swaying and drifting all over the road as they fought for control of the vehicle.

He thought his days were at an end, their short lives coming to a calamitous end... But she was no match for his strength. He took over the wheel. Marcus readdressed it in the correct position, on the proper side of the road.

She tried to fight his hands off. "Are you frightened, Dr. Stewart?" she goaded him. If she would have been able to grasp the heat in his eyes, she'd be afraid, and done exactly what he said.

"Enough!" he cried out, holding on to the steering wheel. He was trying to reach the brake pedal with his foot from the passenger seat, when they heard a siren bellowing loud behind them. Blue flashing lights flooded the countryside in warning.

Black curses erupted from his mouth.

The police, bloody hell! Now what?

Erin didn't understand some of his blasphemes, but she was sure it meant nothing good for her.

"Happy? Stop the damn thing!" he said in a tone seemingly calm, but he was beyond vexed.

She could hear the strain in his voice as he struggled to compose himself, barely achieving it. She dithered for a few more seconds. When the police officer on a motorbike flanked her, pointing to the side of the road, she had no choice. She stopped.

The motorbike halted in front of her. The officer made his way to the car.

While they took a respite, their breathing lowered, their hearts in their throats, thundering fast. The passenger, with relief the car had finally stalled. The driver, with anxiety at what was to happen. Erin waited in trepidation for the officer. She tried not to look at her irate lover in the passenger seat. She was between the sickle and the hammer.

"Dangerous, are we? Are you trying to kill somebody?" the officer said, flashing a light on her. She blinked rapidly, raising a hand to cover her face. "Documents, miss," he asked sharply.

"Arrest me! It's my f-fault. I accept full responsibility. Please t-take me," Erin blabbered in alarm, half stammering and half slurring her words. Her plan ended in a miserable failure. But at least she would be arrested and away from him, anyway. Not how she planned it. But better a jail cell than remaining in the damn clinic, near him.

"Good evening, Tom," Marcus said in an assertive tone.

"Dr. Stewart?" The police officer, shocked, squinted at the doctor, flashing his light on him.

"Yes, Tom " He had regained his self-control and cooled somewhat.

"Sorry, sir, I didn't realise you were in the car. I recognised it, but I thought someone had stolen it. What's going on?"

"May I speak to you for a moment? In private?" He glanced at the young officer with a nod of the head toward her.

"Sure."

He started the engine on for a second and put the headlights on. "That's where they are!" Marcus said to her in a mocking tone. But his eyes were not smiling. He turned the ignition off again, leaving the headlights on, so he could see in the pitch dark and watch her. Then, he yanked the keys out of the ignition. She sought to grab them, but she was a second too late.

"What are you doing?" she asked in a panic and half defiant, but he just glared at her and ignored her question.

"Stay, don't move!" he directed. She bit her bottom lip. Marcus opened the car door.

"I'm not your dog..." she muttered under her breath. He ignored her.

He got out of the car to talk to the officer. They walked away, whispering for five minutes.

Erin was on tenterhooks. What the hell were they whispering about for what looked like an eternity?

"What's happening there?" she yelled at them. "Aren't you going to handcuff me?" she went on, turning her head.

The men came back to her side.

"Good night, miss. Don't do this again. Next time, I will arrest you for dangerous driving, and for doing it under the influence, and God knows I have a few more offences to add to the list. You wasted enough of my time and the doctor's, already!" The officer lectured to her, and then he spun to Marcus. "Doctor, please make sure she doesn't drive anywhere tonight." He turned on his heels and walked towards his motorbike.

"Move, I'll drive," Marcus demanded bluntly of her.

"What?" She leaned her head out of the car, gaping at the young man's retreating figure. "Officer, aren't you going to arrest me? Is that it?"

"Move, I said," Marcus snapped, his patience at an end.

"Oh, for God's sake, you have to jail me. I was driving under the influence," she yelled after the police officer, "come back."

When she heard the roaring of his motorbike, she cursed. The officer left, zooming off on his bike. He disappeared in a flash in the darkness. They were alone again.

She lifted her head to him. She swallowed. Her bottom lip trembled.

Marcus was standing outside the car, towering over her. His hands on his hips, he was fuming. At that moment, he reminded her of a furious bull fit to strike his torero in the ring with all he had. His face appeared calm, inscrutable. Though she grasped he was a thousand miles off from the land of bliss. His vibes were dreadful. He had a strange glint in his eyes. She couldn't completely appreciate the expression in the dark, and in her present state of inebriation and anxiety, she was too scared to read. But she would bet her life, it was not a benevolent expression. What she didn't know was he wanted to blister that pampered, dangerous ass of hers damn hard! Looking at him in her highly charged condition, she didn't quite grasp it.

"Move, and I am not telling you again."

"I'm not going anywhere with you!" she replied with a pout. She tried to get out of the car, but he pushed her back into it unceremoniously. "You beast!" she spat when he thwarted her deed. She scampered to the passenger seat. She tried to get out that way. He was on her in a flash, so she darted across to the driving seat again.

"You are out of line! This is nonsense." He stopped her from leaving the car.

"I am not staying with you, and you cannot make me. I want to be arrested." She moved like a Yo-Yo to the other side.

"You spend too much time with Belinda. Prison is not fun. Tom wanted to arrest you if I had let him. It was hard to convince him," he said, but she didn't listen.

When she gripped the steering wheel, he slapped her hands until she released it. She scampered to the passenger seat again, but he caught up with her. She raced back and forth as he imprecated to the evils of the world that had befallen him with this woman. Erin was trying to run away from him, and he blocked every exit.

At last, she got out of the car from the passenger door. She ran. She didn't go far as he seized her on the side of the road. He grabbed her with his arms around her waist tightly, her back to him.

She swore at him. "Leave me alone!"

"Quiet! You foolish woman!"

"I would rather go to jail than anywhere with you!" She thrashed about, trying to liberate herself.

"Thank your lucky stars it was Tom! Or you were headed to a cell tonight."

"You idiot! You liar!" she screamed at him, cursing him for not releasing her.

He raised her from the ground, her feet dangling. "Quiet!"

"Jerk! Leave me alone. Go to your little nurse," she said as she fought and struggled to free herself, hitting his arms with her fists as he held her tightly to him.

"What?"

"You heard me! Bloody liar!" She kicked his shin, and he cursed, but he didn't relent.

"What the hell are you talking about? Stop struggling. You are drunk and not making any sense."

"You and the nurse... I caught you with Stevenson! Caressing her. You certainly were not keeping your distance from her, were you? You bonehead!"

"Stevenson?" he mumbled, and she dug her nails into his arm. "Ouch, what the hell!"

"Yes, her! I saw you. You pervert! I hate you!" She launched at him. The anguish she'd bottled up for days was now venting on him. She wrestled with him, trying to disentangle herself from his hold. He was behind her, gripping her with his arms around her waist as she wriggled about.

He made any action to extricate herself impossible. She elbowed him in the ribs, hard. He cursed, but his grip on her was powerful. She wasn't going anywhere, and he dragged her back to the car. "You are infuriating! The girl is my niece if you must know!"

"Niece! Niece?" she cried out at the top of her lungs, and she shrieked a long scream. A wolf would not have howled that loud. She thrashed about, hitting him harder, like a hurricane ripping the earth from its contents with the force of nature. She pulled her hands up and tried to pull his hair.

Unrepeatable expletives left his mouth.

She fought him like a demon.

Remarkably, though not happy, he had gained enough of his composure, and went about taming her. "Yes, niece! Stevenson is my niece," he uttered unequivocally. He couldn't believe the woman had turned into a little savage. She had crossed every line.

"I am not an idiot!" she bellowed. "For a clever man, I thought you would come up with a more imaginative excuse. Your niece, my foot! You bloody liar!" And she leaned over, trying to bite his hands, and when she couldn't reach his hand with her mouth, she pinched it and dug her nails into them, too.

"Christ!" he yelled in pain, but his grip on her was fierce. He wouldn't let her get away with this.

"Let me go! I want to go home. I don't wish to be in your fucking clinic anymore."

"Stevenson is my niece, and you are under my care. And you'll do what I tell you. Stop struggling and get in the car. This minute! You've tried my patience to its limit for one night."

"Get off me!"

"It's the truth, woman!"

"Piss off!"

"Erin, your last warning."

"Sod off, Marcus, you lying bastard!"

"Right, that's it. I have had enough of your nonsense." And he flung her over the top of the car's bonnet, face down, none too gently.

She yelped a curse at him. "Pig!"

"You brash, insolent, foul mouthed brat. You could have killed us."

She tried to kick her way out of trouble like a recalcitrant wild horse. Her arms flailing around, trying to hit him.

He stood behind her. He pressed her down, keeping her secured to the bonnet, face down, so she would not move. Marcus pinned her wrists on her back after a brief struggle. She kicked her legs wildly. But her strength was no match for his, in particular in the sombre mood he was in.

She struggled to defend herself. Though, in that position, she could do nothing at all.

With his other hand, he pulled her leggings and panties down to her knees forcefully. He almost ripped them off her, and sidestepping, he proceeded without preamble, to spank her backside. He swung his arm back. His palm aimed for her ass, and when it made contact, it branded her apple cheeks.

She yelped and threw improprieties at him, but the bite of the sting took her breath away. The raw power of his smacks and the perfect placement on the crest of her buttocks made an imprint of his hand on her creamy skin. The heavy sting brought tears to her eyes. Her ass was on fire soon enough. "Ow, ow, stop! We are in the middle of the road. Are you crazy?"

"On a country road, at eleven!"

"People will see us."

"Don't concern yourself. They'll turn the other way when they see it's me." And he smacked her hard.

"Marcus…" she begged, the bite on her posterior unbearable, burning with heat.

"You are in deep trouble! And when I say, deep, that doesn't cover it. Are you going to sit in silence, so we can go home?" And he walloped her derrière with more solid smacks until she could barely talk, in agony. The skin on her backside glowed in the dark. An alien could have spotted her red ass from another planet; it was flaming like a blazing fire.

"That's not home!" she mumbled, inconsolable.

"Erin!" he warned, his spanking more vigorous.

"Please, stop," she pleaded in a whisper. The booming impact of his palm on her skin, reverberated in the pitch-dark on the silent road. Tears were streaming from her eyes. "I promise, stop," she begged in utter misery. But in her present state, her pussy throbbed at his hand on her backside. Even upset with him, she couldn't deny the attraction to him. She wanted him more than anything in the world. Her drenched channel was a testament to him. Under the circumstances, she was mortified and humiliated.

Was it true? Was Stevenson his niece? It could not be! His sister, Dr. Devlin, was way too young to be Stevenson's mother. Besides, Erin had heard from the cook at the clinic Marcus's dead wife had no family. So where had this niece suddenly sprang from? No, it was impossible! *Liar!*

She stopped struggling, worn out, and whimpered. He gave her two more whacks, and when her body went limp with exhaustion, drink and arousal, he paused the spanking.

"Right!" he said, and he pulled her panties and leggings up firmly, but not before he had a good view of her sex and ran his fingers alongside her slit, the temptation too strong.

She moaned, wanting more despite herself. But he would not humour her, not tonight.

His cock had stirred and swelled at the sight of her round, plump, fabulous red butt. "Sit, let's get out of here. And not a word, understood? Not until I give you permission." He pulled her up and released her on her feet again, raising her face to him. He glanced at her, his hand under chin, and he couldn't help wiping her tears from her cheeks with his thumb, caressing her. And he wished with all his might to melt her with kisses.

But then her appalling behaviour flared his blood, dismissing the fleeting moment of passion. "Get in, now!" he ordered with his eyes flaming at her.

She sat in the passenger seat, quietly, as she sniffed some tears, as meek as a lamb, with a sore bottom. She shifted in the seat uncomfortably and there was a hint of a smirk on his face.

"Liar! Liar," she muttered under her breath.

He heard her mumbling but said nothing. At least he had calmed her down. He inspected the big gash on the side of the car. He blurted out a curse.

"Is it too bad?" she simpered, but one look from him shut her up. She realised it was the wrong question at the worst time. Better to be quiet.

As he returned to the driver's door, she couldn't resist one last comment. "Sorry! But this is your fault," she went on pigheadedly, which he ignored with a huff. And it was a good thing he avoided her, otherwise he would have blistered her butt again, then and there. He sat in the driver's seat instead.

He started the car, turned it around and roared off back to the clinic.

They drove in silence.

She gave him furtive glances, but he was a mask. He didn't say a word. She couldn't read him, and the darkness didn't help.

She was praying to the heavens for his normal demeanour, for his calmness to return before they got back.

As they were approaching the clinic, he turned to her. "Don't think we're done. The spanking tonight was not a punishment. Not even the beginning. That was to calm you down, to get you in the car and off the road. I'll deal with your appalling, dangerous behaviour later."

Chapter 14

s they arrived at the clinic and he parked his car by the cottage, his sister came running out of the house.

"God, I was out of my wits with worry about you! Are you okay?" She placed her hands on the car's window. She glanced at her brother then her gaze bounced to Erin.

"We are fine. Not if Miss Blake had anything to do with it, though. She almost killed us," Marcus mumbled through gritted teeth with no further explanation as he raked a hand through his dark hair.

Erin scowled, her old gripe with him and the young nurse still burning her, but she didn't say a word. She had a very sore arse, and she didn't want a repeat. Even if her pussy was still damp because of it.

Dr. Devlin gave a sigh of relief at seeing them well, but she didn't ask for details. She had more urgent issues to deal with.

He was about to exit the car when his sister raised a hand, stopping him in his tracks. "Goran won't wake up. We found him in the reading room. Matron and I pulled him from his chair, walked him along for ten minutes trying to get him going, but he is not responding. Dr. Bell is on night duty. He is with him now. He tried too, but nothing. I called you, but there was no reply on your phone. I wasn't sure if you had taken it with you. I came back to the cottage to check," Julia said. There was concern in her tone, her face a worried mask, a sheen of sweat on her upper lip, and her gaze skipping between the two.

"I-I gave h-him sleeping pills," Erin stammered, barely audible, but owning up to her deed. She swallowed hard. Her head dropped to her chin, and if it weren't for the dark night, they would have seen her checks burn with shame. She wrung her hands in her lap with apprehension for her friend now, not daring to look at the doctors.

"You *what?*" He turned to her, his eyes blazing, and she flushed, mortified with remorse. Even in the dark, she noticed a muscle twitching in his jaw through the corner of her eyes. His countenance darkened. If he was furious before, she was sure he was about to explode like a ticking bomb now. She launched a furtive glance at him, but his face said it all.

Erin crumpled in her seat at his deadly scrutiny. The poignant expression had been enough to send her into a spiral of loathing about herself. She was struggling to keep back the tears, her cheeks flaming hot.

"Which pills? How many did you give him?" his sister asked point blank, her voice calm again.

"Three, just three, the ones you gave me," Erin mumbled, tears gathering in her eyes. She was trying to hold them back desperately.

"Are you sure? Three, not more? He is not waking up," Dr. Devlin insisted and didn't let up. It was not the time for niceties. She was concerned about Goran, and her head shook in disapproval. Erin's tears stained her face despite her efforts not to cry.

"The truth, please!" Marcus snapped, and the chill in his voice made her jump in her seat.

"I swear, only three. Oh, sweet Jesus, is he going to be okay? I am so sorry." She burst into sobs at the thought of having harmed her friend. *Is Goran going to die because of me? What have I done? How could I do this?* Her guilt and shame were unbearable; she wanted the earth to swallow her up.

"Take her inside, give her a cup of tea, and don't let her out of your sight. I'll see to Goran."

"Marcus, I-I…" Erin pleaded, but he would not have it.

"Get out of the car, now. I have no time to waste," he commanded, and Julia opened the car's door and pulled Erin out in a hurry.

The moment she was out of the door, he roared off towards the clinic on the other side of the estate without as much as another word.

SHE STOOD THERE, watching the car leave. It worried her. Goran was sick, and it was her fault. Erin kept pinching the skin on her throat, sniffing with tears.

She looked at the sky and launched a swift prayer to the heavens for her friend. *Sweet Jesus, let Goran be well again. I promise, I'll behave! Please, God, help him, don't let any harm come to him.*

If something happened to her companion, she would never forgive herself. All because she had been jealous of Marcus. She had behaved like a silly child, thrown a tantrum. Marcus was right, she was prone to tantrums. A grown-up woman throwing her toys out of the pram. *Shame on you,* she told herself.

She should have confronted Marcus like a mature woman. Instead, she had taken the simple way out. The coward's way… she had run away, and she loathed herself for it. She could have killed Marcus on the road, too, now that she thought about it. And Goran was ill because her behaviour was childish!

"Come on; let's go in. There is nothing to see. We must wait." Dr. Devlin pulled her by the elbow to Dr. Stewart's cottage.

They went to the kitchen. Julia motioned her to the bench at the table. Erin plopped on the bench, sniffing, teary, her lip quivering. Not to mention, she couldn't sit comfortably yet. The flesh of her backside was still raw and burning. She kept fidgeting on it as if it was on fire.

Julia put the kettle on and made tea. When it was done, she poured two cups. All the while Erin had sat quietly, but Julia could hear her sniffing.

"Here, this will make you feel better. Drink, please." She offered her a cup.

Erin grabbed it and took a small sip.

The doctor slumped on the bench, too. "What is this all about, hey? What's going on?" Julia asked in a soothing voice as she sipped her own tea, sitting next to her.

Erin had another gulp at her cup. It was hot, but she was distraught about everything. She didn't feel the burning on her tongue. Her shaking hands spilt droplets of tea on the counter. "I am so sorry about Goran. He is going to be all right, isn't he? I only wanted him to sleep so I could leave, to make my way out of the estate without raising the alarm. I meant no harm or to cause any trouble." Her tone was pleading. She then burst into tears again.

Dr. Devlin put her arm around her shoulders, trying to comfort her. "Come on. Crying won't help; it's useless. I am sure you didn't mean to harm him. Why the hell did you want to leave the clinic, though? We've been talking about your discharge in a few weeks, so I don't understand, and I thought you and my brother…"

"I am sorry to put you through this, Julia. Will he get better? Goran, I mean," Erin called the doctor by her Christian name for the first time, and the young woman smiled at her.

"I don't know, but if anyone can help him, he is in expert hands with Marcus."

"Oh, sweet Jesus. I am hopeless!"

"But why? When your release is imminent, in a few weeks? I don't understand. Why all these shenanigans?" Dr. Devlin asked her with a shocked, pained expression. Somehow, she felt hurt that Erin had not confided in her about whatever was upsetting her.

"I-I…"

"What is it? What happened?" Dr. Devlin wished to find out what had motivated her to this ludicrous exploit.

"Well, I…"

"Tell me. You know you can say anything to me," she said with compassion, sensing how upset her patient was. The psychiatrist was at a loss at this unforeseen erratic behaviour from Erin. Why would she do such a foolish thing? She worried for her patient and wanted to understand what had triggered it. The doctor was certain she was past that phase now, but this sudden relapse troubled her. Besides, Julia was quite fond of her, and she had no doubt her brother was too.

"I saw them," Erin whispered, and a sob escaped her.

"Who?"

"Marcus and Stevenson!" She wiped her tears with the back of her hand.

"Stevenson?" Dr. Devlin repeated in an unusually high tone. "I don't understand?"

"Aha, I caught them. He kissed the top of her head."

"You mean Nurse Stevenson?"

"Yes, her! The bastard! Sorry, I know he is your brother, but he lied to me. He told me he loved me when all the time, he and the young nurse…"

"He told you he loves you? You saw Marcus with Clara?"

"Yes. That's her name, isn't it? Yes, Clara, I did."

"Marcus and Clara?"

"Yes!" Erin shouted fervently while the woman chuckled. Why would this clever doctor not understand what she was saying to her?

"Umm…" Julia scoffed and a small smile formed on her lips.

"I tell you, it's true. He had his arm around the nurse's shoulder with an idiotic grin on his face. That means one thing. Love! He kissed the top of her head. Does he kiss all his nurses like that, ha? Stevenson held his hand with hers, on her shoulders. You know what that means, don't you? Marcus is not as upright as he thinks he is, nor too worried about his reputation now, is he? It was all an excuse for me." Erin burst into tears again, covering her face with her hands. She cried so much that her eyes turned red and puffy. She sniffed and needed to wipe her nose.

"I need a hanky. I lost mine," she mumbled, weeping like a baby.

Dr. Devlin sighed. She left the kitchen to get a box of tissues from the study. She gave her a couple when she returned to the room.

Erin took them and blew her nose but couldn't stop crying and sniffing, muttering to herself, "I saw them, I did!" over and over as if in a hellish chant.

"You must love him to do these foolish things. Do you? He's right when he calls you a silly poppet," Julia said, shaking her head in disapproval.

Her eyes snapped back to the doctor's. "I do love him. I adore him. Does he really call me that?" She stopped crying when she realised what the doctor had said. "But you see why I can't stay here, knowing what's going on with Stevenson?"

"Dear me, Erin. You foolish woman! Marcus is her uncle; didn't he tell you?" Julia told her with impatience.

"His niece? I know his wife had no family; the cook told me once. And you can't possibly be the young nurse's mom, you are too young, surely!"

"No, I am not. I am her aunt, darling. She is our oldest brother's girl. Charles died twenty years ago in an accident. We didn't know he'd left a daughter until she was twelve. When Clara's mother was ill, she came looking for us. With no family and with Clara still a child, we were her only hope. The woman passed away soon after that. The girl has no one but us. We are her family."

"Oh, God!" Erin gasped. She didn't realise there was a brother.

"The girl doesn't wish people to know she is our niece. Clara doesn't want other staff thinking her job here is due to favouritism. She lives in town, quite an independent young woman she is, our niece. She looks up to him. The girl worships him. He is the only father she has ever known. Marcus and his wife, poor soul, never had children. They were going to adopt her. Then Penny got ill… Well, he dotes on her as if she were his own daughter. Certainly not in the way you mean, dear."

"Ooh… God! He mentioned it, b-but I-I…" She sniffed, teary, the realisation of the enormity of her mistake hitting her, and tears came down her face.

"You didn't believe him."

"No…" She shook her head, and more tears streaked her cheeks.

Though Marcus had told her the same, in her obstinacy, Erin had not believed him, not trusted him. Now she had to face the truth... she had messed everything up.

"Erin, we talked about this for so long. I thought you were getting over your trust issues. You've got to trust people, trust Marcus," Dr. Devlin said with compassion, caressing her hair.

"I adored my twin brother, but I couldn't count on him. He did bad things. He promised he wouldn't do them, but he always did. I couldn't trust him."

"Darling, Marcus is not your brother. He is a good person. You've got to have faith in him."

"I know, b-but—"

"If Marcus told you he loved you, he meant it. He wouldn't say a thing like that willy-nilly if he wasn't in love with you. You need to learn to count on him, to trust him. He'll be hurt you didn't."

"Oh, God, I've screwed up everything!"

"No, you haven't. He knows why you are here, and amongst other things, the problems with your trust issues. He'll understand and will forgive you. Perhaps, not tonight, but he will," Dr. Devlin stated with a sweet smile.

The revelation gave her, on one hand, a great relief. On the other, she felt contrition at the way she had behaved with him for no reason at all, not trusting him, not believing in him.

Sweet Jesus, I am such a fool! There was no end to her foolishness, Marcus was right, she realised. If there was a Nobel Prize for silliness, for irrationality, she would win it.

She always ruined everything, and she had botched her chances with Marcus. What a mess!

"We loved our brother, and Clara is all we have left of him. She is so dear to us. You'll adore her, too. I'm sure," Dr. Devlin said as she caressed her hair.

Erin tried to dry some tears out of her wet, dull eyes after all that crying. She covered her face with her hands in shame briefly before pulling them away. She'd made a big mess of things.

How will I look into his eyes again? He'll hate me after this. And I may have killed poor Goran, too! What a disaster!

"Oh, God!" Erin wept uncontrollably. Dr. Devlin tried to console her, but there was no soothing her. She bit her bottom lip, chewing it, ravaging the wretched flesh, the enormity of her misguided actions hitting her in full blow.

Julia made some more tea and prepared her a sandwich. Erin sipped the tea, but she couldn't eat a morsel. She was distraught, and Dr. Devlin thought the girl was going to pass out in agony. So, the doctor gave her a sedative to calm her down.

The phone rang, and Julia answered. She spoke briefly to the person on the line while Erin tried to listen, but she couldn't make heads or tails of the medical conversation.

"Was it your brother?" she asked when the discussion ended.

Dr. Devlin nodded.

"What's wrong with Goran? Did he say?"

"Marcus pumped his stomach. So, all the pills are out of Goran's system. Though, by themselves, they shouldn't have been enough to harm him. Perhaps there was some kind of unforeseen reaction to them. Then, he used a counteractive medication to the sleeping tablets. It reverses the sedation caused by them. He brought him back to his normal state, or as close to it as he could be under the circumstances. Goran will be in a daze for a while. We'll monitor his progress and recovery over the next few hours, although it may be a day or two before he is himself again. But he'll be okay," Dr. Devlin said with a soothing smile.

"Thank God!" Erin was so relieved, she scrambled out of her seat and crushed Julia into a bear-hug, crying on her shoulders. "Can I see him?"

"No. Perhaps tomorrow. We'll see. He needs to rest. And you go to bed, too, on my brother's orders. The sedative will work its magic soon on you and help you sleep."

"I'll go to my room, to the clinic."

"No, it's late. Marcus said for you to settle in his guest bedroom for tonight."

"Oh no, I couldn't." She shook her head with a blush.

"Yes, my sentiments exactly," Dr. Devlin emphasised, and Erin launched her a hurtful glance, but she thought she deserved it after what she had done.

"I'll walk to the clinic then," she replied sheepishly.

"No. You are to stay here; those are his orders. What I mean is fuck the guest room! Go to his bedroom instead; stay in his bed. It's obvious the two of you love each other, and you are both behaving like silly teenagers. Get on with it. Take a good rumble in bed with him!" Julia winked with a mischievous grin.

"What?" Erin blinked rapidly at the outspoken comment from the doctor. It was unexpected.

"Don't look so shocked." The young woman raised her brows. "My brother has been impossible for months since you arrived. And worse since Mollie's party! It's about time if you ask me."

"Fine, I'll take the guest room, Dr. Devlin, then."

"Oh, Julia is fine, Erin, don't you think?" They smiled at each other. "Are you sure you don't want my brother's room instead?"

"For now, it's better if I keep my distance from Marcus. If I wish to keep on living after what I've done tonight," she scoffed, somewhere between the serious and facetious.

"You may have a point there! He is not happy."

MARCUS RETURNED TO HIS COTTAGE. It was almost daybreak by then. He was exhausted, hungry, and cold. He had worked long hours the previous day and had been tired by evening to start with. When Erin's drama unfolded, with the consequences of chasing her on the road and then having to provide emergency medical attention to Goran until then, the entire hullabaloo had shattered him. He was drained, not to mention the emotional aftermath.

Thank God, Goran will be fine. The woman could have killed him. Well, she could have killed both of us, too, with her bloody erratic drive, the minx! There is no end to her silliness. Jesus, she needs a good talking to, a stern one at that! Not tonight, though, I am too tired for it. She'll have to wait until the morning.

He stepped into the sitting room. His sister was asleep on his couch. He covered her with a throw. She'd been waiting for him to return. He had asked her not to leave Erin alone, and she'd stayed.

He got a glass of water from the kitchen. But he couldn't let his sister sleep there like that. So, he returned to the sitting room. "Julia, wake up." He patted her cheek gently. He sat on the corner of the sofa.

She opened her eyes. "Marcus! What's wrong?" Her face in alarm, she questioned him as she sat up.

"Nothing. All is well." He smiled at her.

In some ways, Julia was still a child to him, even at twenty-seven. He was so much older than she was, but they supported each other. He had nursed her through a painful divorce eighteen months ago, not long after his wife, Penny, had died. His sister was like a little trouper, taking everything bravely, his wife's death, her divorce.

Julia had married young and became a doctor while married, thus accounting for why she still used Devlin as her last name instead of Stewart. Marcus hoped she would ditch it one day and let go of her past, of her marriage, forever. The sweet darling had dedicated herself to her job at the clinic, trying to forget all else. She deserved to be happy, but so far, she had not been too lucky with men.

He sighed. He'd looked after his sister and his niece for so many years. And now, it seemed, he'd have another woman to look after, too. This new one, Erin, would not be so easy to manage, *certainly not very obedient!* he thought with a furrowing brow after the shenanigans of last night.

"Are you sure?"

"At the clinic, yes. Matron and Dr. Bell will take turns looking after Goran until the day shift shows up in the morning. They'll pick up from there. The worst is passed. He is resting now. He'll be fine in a couple of days," Marcus said, giving her a curt nod of confirmation.

"I'm so glad to hear it!"

"You should get some rest, too, Julia. Go home and go to bed. I have told Matron to request two doctors to stand in for us tomorrow. You won't be in a condition to work after the night we had. Take the day off. That's an order. I'll look in on Goran in the afternoon. They know to call me if there are any changes."

"What time is it?" his sister asked.

"It's gone four am. Bed, come on," he said, displaying a small smile.

"You, too, Marcus. You need some rest," she urged, but he scoffed and rolled his eyes.

"Don't you worry about me." He glanced around but did not ask about the other woman.

His sister realised what he wished to know. "Erin is upstairs in your guest bedroom. I gave her a sedative. She was too distraught," Julia stated with a pained expression on her face.

"Did you tell her about Goran?"

"Yes. She was overjoyed he is going to be fine and crushed me into a bear hug." Julia laughed and went on, "She's explained the reason for all this silliness. You see, she thought of you and Clara—"

"I know, the reckless woman, God, she has some trust issues!" His brow furrowed with a deep crease in between.

"Erin loves you, Marcus," she whispered, her features softening on him, glad her brother had a new woman.

"Umm… what a way to show it," he spat, but she put a hand on his arm. It was a soothing gesture.

"Deep down, she is a creature of spirit. But she worships you, she—"

"Fine, fine. Don't worry about her now; leave her to me." He stood up, showing the conversation about his woman was at an end.

"But Marcus, Erin—"

"Enough, go to bed." He reached out for her, raised her from the sofa, and walked her to the hall. He then helped her put her coat on and kissed the top of her head.

"Go, I'll watch you until you get inside your cottage," he urged and opened the front door.

The cool, early morning breeze blew in, making them blink. It refreshed them, lifting some sleep from their heavy eyelids. They both breathed in.

"You'll be nice to her, won't you, be gentle?" she warned him in a scowl.

He laughed and patted her nose with his finger. He kissed her on the forehead and shoved her gently out of the door. "Come on, shoo, bed!" And he ambled with her to the gate of his cottage.

His sister scoffed and rolled her eyes.

He stood there watching her go until she reached her cottage, on the other side of the gates to the estate. She waved back at him before she disappeared inside. He gave a sigh of relief, moved back inside, and locked the door. He needed some time alone.

He went to his study and got himself a brandy. The coveted brandy he'd never gotten the chance to drink earlier in the evening. He plopped in the armchair by the fireplace, but he drained the liquid in two gulps. He was too restless. Marcus rose and poured himself another one. This time, he savoured it with more delight and less pace. He couldn't get Erin off his mind, only a staircase separating her from him. He placed the glass down on the low table with a thud and made his way up the stairs. He listened outside her bedroom. There was no sound. He opened the door quietly and went in. He leaned on the doorframe, his eyes adjusting to the darkness. A moonbeam cast through the window flickered a silvery light, and he could now see her shape in bed. He came to stand in the middle of the room, watching her.

She stirred after a minute. "Marcus, is that you?" Erin mumbled, still half asleep. She reached for the bedside lamp and turned it on. She blinked, sat up in bed, gave him a small, coy smile, and flushed.

He didn't return her smile, but his eyes betrayed him. There was a glint in them. The sight of her in a short camisole warmed the cockles of his heart despite his dismal humour and her horrendous behaviour. She looked so pretty with her dark, long hair tumbling about her, sitting up in bed. Her skin glowing in the silvery light.

"How is Goran?" she mumbled with a concerned look.

"He'll be fine. We'll monitor him for a few days," he said, and then he puffed a breath of air out, forcefully. He sounded worn out. His hair was matted, his clothes wrinkled and dishevelled from the busy night.

Erin felt distraught for him, he looked so tired and exhausted. She had caused this. It was her fault. She wished she could cuddle him to sleep in her arm, soothing him, caressing him.

"I am so sorry, Marcus, for everything," she uttered the words as her cheeks burned with emotion and shame, her bosom heaving.

"Are you?" he asked, and for an instant, despite his frustration, he had the impulse to kiss her, to ravish that silly, pouty mouth of hers senseless. That irritated him even more. He would not succumb to her so easily. If he did, she'd think she had him wrapped around her little finger at her will. Oh, no! He would let her stew in her own remorse, in her own guilt, for tonight. Be it a lesson to her.

"I am. Your sister told me... about Clara."

"Did she?"

"Please forgive me. I promise, I'll never do anything like that again," she pleaded and lowered her head on her chin, mortified, when he glared at her.

"Is that so?"

"I don't know how I could let this happen; I apologise!" she muttered under her breath.

"Oh, I do. You are foolish! That's how." He was feeling too raw to let her get away with it too easily.

"Sorry."

"How is it you believed my sister when she told you about Clara, and you didn't believe me? Ha! You don't trust me! Is that it? You have no faith in me, in us."

"Oh, I should have. I am truly sorry." It devastated her. He looked drained after the busy and crazy night, but she felt awful for hurting him with her outlandish recriminations.

"You behaved foolishly, placing your life at risk and that of others. Three people could have died tonight! We were lucky there was no one on the roads. Not to bring up your ridiculous accusations," he sentenced, and his tone told her how much she had upset him. His eyes were dark with a strange emotion.

"I am mortified." A tear came down her face, and she wiped it with her hand.

"You and your outbursts are a handful. I won't tolerate this behaviour, do you understand? You were a danger to yourself and to others. You should ask questions before you get yourself in such scrapes and strops. If you had talked to me, trusted me, none of this would have happened." The scowl on his face emphasised the rebuke in his tone and words as he chastised her.

"I didn't realise you had a brother. I'm sorry I didn't believe you, that I didn't trust you. I know I should have. Will you forgive me?"

"You think it's that simple? You are too impulsive. Next time use your brain before you act."

"I will; I am sorry."

"Stop repeating that. You mumble an apology and reckon that's it? Assume all is forgiven? You almost killed us in my car and nearly damned succeeded in killing Goran, too, with your stupid idea. Just luck you didn't! It is a shameful behaviour, and I won't have it. Understood?"

"Yes," she murmured but could not hold his glare. She blushed but could not avert a furtive peek at him, her desire stirring under his chastisement, under his deadly scrutiny. Even with a dark expression on his face, he aroused her. Her pussy became wet, and she tightened her legs closed. It would disgrace her further if he knew he was arousing her now by scolding her. She needed all her self-control to stop herself from running into his arms.

"And one more thing. Is this the reason you were wearing the red dress the other night? The one I forbade you to wear? Hmm... no lies, please."

"Uh... ah?" She wouldn't dare glance at him and wrung her hands on her lap.

"Come on; is it?" he pressed when she didn't answer.

"Yes." She peeked at him with misty eyes, embarrassed, humiliated at her exploits with the dress. If the room had been lighter, she would have seen a little nerve twitch in his cheek. His already set jaw clenched, his teeth grinding. He was still furious with her, and the issue with the damn dress didn't help.

"I need some rest. I have no energy to deal with you tonight. I'll bank this. In the meantime, think of what you've done, of how you are going to make amends, and never do it again. Go back to sleep." And he pivoted on his heels and left.

She turned on her pillow and cried. He would not forgive her.

Chapter 15

After a shower and another brandy, he went to bed. He fell asleep the second his head hit the pillow, but he'd awakened with a start not too long after. Marcus dreamt about her, about caressing her in that tiny, silk camisole. In his dream he made love to her, riding her roughly, and ravishing her with his kisses.

Now awake… Jesus, he was as hard as a rock and so close to coming, his dick ached. He hadn't had this kind of wet dreams for years. It had happened in his youth once or twice, but here he was again, because of Erin, and it wasn't the first time, either, since she'd landed in his clinic.

Bloody hell, she will be my undoing…

What was it about this woman that caused his blood to swoosh in his veins faster, hotter? That raised his pulse so frantically that it made him want her with all his soul and body? For the life of him, he couldn't say. His visceral attraction had turned into love for her over the last few months, and he wanted her in his life. The damned cheeky girl, in all her glory and with all her faults! God knew, he had a few of his own; they were a good match!

He grunted in frustration. *She'll either kill me or drive me mad.* Marcus wasn't sure which would come first, but he had to deal with her and her appalling, reckless behaviour. She was a handful, willful and unpredictable. Erin could be as timid as a mouse, as gentle as a rose petal, as sweet and beautiful as a nymph, as sexy as a siren. She could be a clever enchantress, then suddenly explode and turn into a wild demon. She didn't listen to reason when she got something into her head, and she had trust issues, in particular about him. She was the embodiment of a woman, and she was all his.

He would have a tough time managing her, but he liked a challenge. Bloody hell, he wouldn't want her any other way. He cursed aloud several times as the realisation hit him. He adored the minx from Hell. He would have to discipline her, though, often, until she realised he would not allow her to adopt certain behaviours. She could be too wild, dangerous. He couldn't tolerate danger, for herself or others, to run amuck with him, wrap him around her little finger.

He would enjoy mastering her. Marcus was sure, below all her high spirits when she got into a temper, she would oblige him in the end. *To please me!* He had an inkling that despite her untamed character, she wanted to be mastered by him. She'd proven it to him that night in Mollie's home, in his office a few weeks ago, and even last night, when she was thrashing around like a wild cat. The spanking did it; it calmed her.

She would never admit it to herself that she liked to be spanked, let alone to him. Jesus, he would blister her ass for the mess she caused. She wouldn't escape him! He had to be firm on that.

God knows, Goran had been touch and go for a while. He thanked his lucky stars that nothing had happened to the young fellow. Not to mention, she destroyed his convertible single-handedly. The gearstick grated and ranted. There was a gash on the entire right side of the damn car. He huffed and cursed. He grabbed his watch from his bedside table; it was 6:30. He tossed and turned for a while in bed. When he realised sleep would not find him again, he got up. He was too restless.

Marcus had a mountain of paperwork waiting for him in his study, patients' notes to write, schedules to define, accounts to deal with. At least he could catch up with work. So, he stepped to the bathroom.

A hand job was necessary in the shower as if he were a horny teenager, given his wet dream about Erin was still vivid in his mind and he still had an aching erection. It dismayed him, but he soon dismissed it. He was a doctor and a practical fellow. These things happened to the best of many.

He was working in his study by seven. About half an hour later, he heard some noises. He opened the door and poked his head in the corridor. Someone was singing. He followed the sound to the kitchen and stopped dead in the doorframe.

Erin was near the stove, dressed in one of his shirts, which barely covered her gorgeous ass, her long-legged limbs on display and her feet bare. She was shapely, curvy in all the right places, and statuesque. She was a tall woman, and there was a lot of her. Against the light from the window, he could see her bountiful silhouette underneath the thin material, and his cock stirred.

She had her back to him, ministering to what looked like scrambled eggs on the cooker. She mixed them with a spatula. Erin didn't notice his presence; she had headphones on, with music in her ears. She added some milk to the pan, while she hummed in harmony to something on her headpiece.

He liked her tone, singing in a soft, melodious, and harmonious voice. It gave him goosebumps. He smiled, but he could not hear the original song as it was on her headphones, for her amusement only. The tune was familiar. He couldn't make out what it was.

Suddenly, she started dancing while she sang, the rubber spatula from the eggs in her hand as she swayed and sang.

He stared at her in wonderment, half amused and well aroused, his head high, his eyes focused on her and engaged in her merriment, following her every movement. His cock throbbed. Marcus noticed the long, silky expanse of creamy skin that were her beautiful legs, moving rhythmically. She shook her plump, round ass to the tune, and he bit his bottom lip.

He leaned his shoulder on the doorframe, crossed his arms on his chest and his right ankle over his left, and enjoyed the show with laughter in his eyes.

God, that's my woman! Make no mistake, she belongs to me. She always has, even when she didn't know it. A possessive streak for her arose from his soul and awakened his blood. Marcus loved watching her dance until she did a pirouette in a move and saw him.

"Good morning," he said as a grin spread from ear to ear. Her little performance had calmed him. His shoulders relaxed for the first time since last night's events. He beamed at her.

HIS GREY EYES twinkled at her with a playful glint, and the smile on his lips gave him a sexy look.

Erin's breath caught in her throat at the beauty of the man. "Marcus!" she shrieked after a moment. She tore the earphones from her head and deposited them on the table.

"Well, that was quite a show," he rumbled and coughed to disguise his arousal.

She turned as red as a fire engine. "How long have you been standing there?"

"Long enough." He grinned. "And what is it you are doing in my kitchen, may I ask?"

"Making you breakfast."

"You don't have to do that."

"I know, but I want to do it. It's the least I can do after last night," she mumbled, peeking at him with a soft expression. "Besides, you mentioned I should think of ways to make amends. This is one of them."

"Umm? One of them? Have you considered others?" He raised an eyebrow, but she ignored him.

"Ahem…" She flushed. Oh, yes, she had considered other ways to make it up to him, and mostly, they included ways in which her body wrapped around his.

"I wonder!" He had an impish grin on his face. The dance had put him in a good mood, despite everything.

"Breakfast will be ready in two minutes. I made all your favourites," she said, defusing a moment of sexual innuendos.

"Uh? How would you know about my favourites?" he asked, firing her a dubious look.

"I have been observing you getting breakfast, lunch, and dinner for four months, in the dining room. I have a good idea by now of what you like."

"You looked at my tray?"

"So? Not a crime, is it?" She sulked.

He grinned.

Sweet Jesus, he is so handsome when he smiles. He should do it more often.

"Wait, a minute! There was nothing in my fridge. Where did you get all that stuff?"

"I went to the big kitchen at the clinic while you had a shower."

"Oh, God! You said it was for me? Did anyone see you? Do you know what that means, now?" He blurted the string of questions as his eyes darkened, with a wrinkle between his brows. Of course, his staff would have seen her. They were preparing for another busy day.

"Oh, grow up, Marcus! I guess the young police officer last night, what was his name?"

"Tom."

"He didn't quite keep the incident to himself, did he?"

"What do you mean?"

"Well, his mother is the cook in the clinic, isn't she?"

"Yes, Winnie!" he huffed and closed his eyes, knowing what would come next. "What of it? That's how I kept you from a police cell last night. You would have gotten arrested. So, count your lucky stars Tom has the highest admiration for me and the clinic. I've helped his family along over the years, so he returned a favour. But he was clear on one thing. If he finds you again in the condition you were last night, anywhere near a car, he'll arrest you on the spot. And not even God will prevent him from doing it next time. Understood, missy?"

"Yes," she mumbled and nodded with her head vigorously, rather embarrassed at her shenanigans.

"What about Winnie then? She is his mother."

"I am glad the young officer is keeping this in the family, then. When I went to the kitchen this morning to borrow the eggs and bits and pieces for breakfast, Winnie said, *'Oh poor Dr. Stewart, he won't like what you did to his car. But he will forgive you, Miss Blake. We are all taking bets on you and the doctor. I am sure it won't be long before you'll be a permanent resident at the cottage, miss, everyone expects so.'* Ahem… That's word for word, Marcus, do you get it now? I was shocked! But there you have it."

"She said that? Tom told her about last night, I can't believe it!" he huffed. "And dressed like that, I am not surprised," he retorted as he pulled a hand through his hair.

"Don't you see? You are the only one who thinks no one knows about us. They are taking bets! And no, I had my coat over your shirt."

"JESUS!" He looked at her. The crease between his brows deepened, knowing his love-life, the little there was of it, was by now the talk of the clinic. Perhaps the gossip had reached town, too, if he were to hazard a guess. *For heaven's sake!* That was exactly what he was trying to avoid.

Then she smiled at him. The sweetest one, a bit coy, somewhat defiant and sheepish, and his heart melted in the warmth of her beam. He rolled his eyes and smiled back with a huff. *The hell with everything! Who cares! Let them gossip!* He finally gave in.

"Besides, I had to borrow your shirt because I seem to have only my toiletries bag. I am not sure what happened to my clothes. I don't know where my other bags are. I looked in your car and they are not there."

"I see," he mumbled. *Oops.* Marcus had a vague recollection from last night of him throwing her bags out on the road with fury as the car sped, with him twirling in all directions in the backseat. *Umm...* an unwitting retribution for her unacceptable behaviour. A corner of his mouth curved on one side. *I'll have to buy her new clothes.* For now, it suited him to have her in his shirt.

"You'll help me find them later, won't you? Or I shall have to visit Goran like this."

"Leave him alone. He's feeling better but resting. I don't want you to bother him," he said with a warning glance, "and you are going nowhere dressed like that."

"I need to talk to him—" she said, but he shook his head with another warning.

"No!"

"Anyway, breakfast is ready. Come; tuck in," she went on, without insisting about Goran, not wanting to argue. She placed the cutlery on the breakfast counter and a plate with toast, butter and jam on the side. Erin poured two cups of steamy fresh coffee, the aroma permeating the room. She dished out the tempting, mouth-watering food, a full, earthy breakfast.

"Well? Are you going to look at it or eat? Come on." She beckoned him with her hand, and they sat next to each other.

"It smells good, and it looks delicious." Marcus was starving. He tucked into his plate of eggs, bacon, tomato, and sausage with a few "mms and ahhs."

Other than that, they ate in companionable silence. He was hungry after the events of the previous night. His shoulders and jaw relaxed even more while he wolfed down his meal. His face was lighting up as he savoured the delicacies on his plate. He was mellowing. He glanced at her with soft eyes, tiny, gratified sighs, and little loving smiles as he devoured his scrambled eggs and ate with gusto.

And she thought, *I'll be dammed, it is true! The way to a man's heart is through his stomach. One of them, anyway. I feed his belly, and he's rediscovering his love for me in his soul? Wow!*

"Delicious," he said with his mouth full. He was enjoying his meal that was cooked by her, for him, lovingly! It felt cozy.

She smiled with satisfaction, her heart melting at having pleased him, for once.

He tilted his head to one side, then this way and that, watching her eat with a grin on his face, as if his mind was processing a thought or seeing something for the first time.

"I am glad you like it," she said, blushing at his obvious inspection.

"This was great. I needed it," he said as he rubbed his tummy when he had finished.

As they rested in silence for a moment, they both reached out for the pot of coffee. His hand grazed hers, but she grabbed it first. He didn't pull his back. He leaned over and played with her shirt collar for a second, adjusting it, sending a bolt of lust to her pussy. Her face flushed, and she became warm.

"Would you like some more coffee?" she asked, and he nodded. As she poured him a cup, she hummed the melody to avoid lustful thoughts about him.

"What are you humming? I know the song. It's the same one you were singing when I came in." And as his hand left her shirt collar alone, he played with a lock of her glossy, cascading hair, knotting and unknotting it around his fingers for a while, until he tucked it away. His fingertips brushed the curve of her ear as he did so.

She had butterflies in her tummy. Her pussy was doing a routine of tightening exercises. It clenched eagerly, preparing herself to welcome him. Her bosom heaved, her breathing lowered. She was soon soaked down below as he caressed her face with his fingertips.

"It's Electric Love. I love it. Do you want to hear it?" she mumbled rapidly, and she took her phone from the counter for something to do as she was getting nervous at his little touches and her increasing arousal. She looked at her phone and searched for it on her playlist. The song blasted out.

"I know it." He smiled. "I liked it, and you sing it well," he said, while she blushed at the compliment.

"What about the dancing?" *Why on earth would I ask him this? What is wrong with me?* she thought to herself.

"WHAT?" he repeated and laughed.

"Did you like it when I was twirling around and singing? George taught me to dance… well, just the one move." Erin had to say something as she embarked onto that conversation with a blush.

"Did he now! Yes, I remember, scandalous!" he rebuked half in jest and half seriously.

"Scandalous?" she scoffed. "That's how young adults dance these days, Marcus. Here, come, let me show you. Dance with me," she proposed with trepidation. She got up from the table, offered her hand to him, raising the volume of the melody. Suddenly, she felt daring and craved the man in that kitchen, right now!

With a glint in her dark moons, inviting him, tempting him, he could not miss her allure. He listened to the sound of the music. His focus darted from her extended palm to her face to her eyes, which were beckoning him.

He followed her lead and took her hand, and Erin made a few dance moves, her long legs moving and her hips swaying in his shirt, barely covering her ass. And his cock had no chance. It stirred and wanted a part in whatever was happening in that kitchen.

She mesmerised Marcus. As if he were a sailor, answering the enchanted, amorous call of a siren, and she were Circe, the sorceress in Homer's Odyssey. Like Odysseus, the humble human hero, he could not prevent the allure of the enchantress on him. He, Marcus, could not resist the burning spell Erin had cast on him long ago. And by means of her incantations, she was luring him into a dangerous, sensual dance that would only end up one way, with the heat of their bodies sizzling. Though, if he were honest, he was counting on that outcome. If truth be told, he wished it, desired it. Each little cell in his body called out to love her, to have her. It demanded it of him. Like a boy in a sweet shop, he wanted to have another bite of the candy. He wanted to taste her sweetness again.

"Follow what I do; you'll be fine," she said, and he laughed, delighting in her taking control.

She took his other hand, recalling what George had told her about the dancing. "Put your arm around my waistline, come as close as you can to me," she whispered, knowing full well what that would do to her insides and to him, her pussy already pulsating in anticipation.

"Like this?" he replied, circling her waist with a powerful arm and pulling her to him with a hard tug. Her body crashed to his chest, and she gasped.

Marcus's eyes glinted, emanating a vibe that said, *oh how I want you!* The pupils of his grey eyes were huge in wonderment and darkened considerably.

She quivered, so close to him. She inhaled the scent of his hair and his zesty essence mixed with his masculinity. It was a powerful aphrodisiac that sent her senses into a meltdown, warning lights flashing, but she didn't care. Butterflies crashed into her tummy.

He caressed her face with his knuckles. She leaned into him, determined to take the lead on the dancing. "Relax, darling."

"Trust me, poppet, I am," he breathed in a low, silvery baritone in her ear. The purring of his voice sent chills through her spine and hit something forceful between her legs. She swallowed hard and put her arms around his collar.

"Now, shut your eyes," she said, looking up at him, wanting to recreate the sexy dance with Marcus, the man she loved.

"Closed!" he uttered with a wicked smile, enjoying her sexiness and delighting in her.

"Tune in to the music, nothing else," she replied, remembering what George had said to her. "Clear your mind. Listen to the sound. Can you do that? Hear the rhythms," she murmured, not quite calm herself. At his proximity, the warmth between her legs swelled across her entire body. Heat surged violently through her and rose by many degrees. Her pussy clenched, and her tummy did a somersault.

His hands slid through her shapely outline, caressing her curvy, well-defined hips, embracing her adorable feminine figure. He wrapped his arms around her waistline and squeezed her tight to him. "I am. What about you? Can you hear it, darling?" he asked smoothly, in a soothing silvery tone. He was tall and imposing, his shoulders wide. He moved her with him, full of confidence, taking control of the dance.

"Y-yes," she stammered, biting her bottom lip, and he fidgeted with the collar of her shirt again, adjusting it as he looked into her eyes.

He inhaled her scent. "Relax, darling. Dance with me; abandon yourself in my arms." He twirled her around the floor. "God, I can't get enough of the scent of your skin, my love. You are stunning," he muttered in her ear as he moved to the music.

Suddenly, it was she who was following his body as he swayed her around the room. He had taken over. She had an inkling Marcus was not a novice at this type of dancing, as he pretended to be. He had just humoured her.

Erin followed the movement of his body with hers, in perfect sync and with rhythm, as the song bellowed out of her phone. They twirled and swayed in the kitchen as he kissed her cheek with a small lick of his tongue, and he brushed his lips from her mouth all the way to the hollow of her neck with tiny little kisses. Her head inclined to one side to expose more of herself to him, to give him better access, sending her into a delirium of lust. She couldn't contain some pitchy, short squeals coming out of her lips as he worked on the sensitive spot on her neck and beyond, until he reached her mouth again.

He twirled to the song with her in his arms, without breaking the kiss, ravishing her, his tongue tasting her, commanding her to open, and she revelled in it. They kissed, over and over, as they swayed to the beat, their lips entwined, their tongues making love to each other.

His cock bulged as her voluptuous breasts scraped his chest with the dance, and even through the material of his shirt, he could feel her pert nipples. His shaft wanted some attention, solid as a rock.

Her pussy drenched. He put his big hands on her plump ass. He grabbed it hard, and she yelped with seduction and some lingering soreness from last night's spanking.

He lifted her from the floor. Marcus held her up, his hands under her bum.

She wrapped her legs around his hips and gave out a naughty laugh. "Oh, I missed you," she mumbled and brushed her lips on his cheek.

"If everyone is talking about us, we may as well give them a good reason for it!" He twirled with her one more time before making a beeline up the stairs to his bedroom with her in his arms.

She squealed all the way.

He deposited her on her feet, his eyes blazing desire at her, with a seductive small grin that sent her pussy on overdrive, in anticipation of what came next. He leaned over her for a kiss, ravishing her mouth, undoing her shirt.

"Oh," she murmured when she felt his cock, rock solid, push on her tummy.

He kissed every bit of skin as he unbuttoned the shirt and slid it from her body, and it crumpled down on the floor.

"You have no underwear!" he blurted with his eyes wide, and she put her arms around his neck and pulled him to her for a kiss to distract him from her missing smalls.

His mouth crashed on hers with the force of his craving and desire. When she was thoroughly kissed, he touched her slit, teasing her opening, and she moaned.

"You are soaked, darling," he whispered with a rough edge to his voice, "do you want me, my love, hmm?" He walked her to the bed. He nudged her back to lie on it, and him with her. He slipped his fingers inside her, and she arched her body to him, but he pressed her back. "I guess that's a yes." He smiled. Marcus pressed her hips down as his fingers sunk in and then out of her gleaming pussy.

"Please..." she was pleading for release, but he removed them, point blank, and she complained.

He moved back and stood up. His feet were on the floor at the edge of the bed.

"Don't move," he said, his eyes scorching her with want. He removed his shoes, socks and shirt.

She smiled at him. His powerful chest with taut muscles came bare before her and she licked her lips. "Marcus," she replied, beckoning him with her eyes and a soft purr of his name.

A mischievous smile formed on his lips and his eyes twinkled. He grabbed her upper arm, lifted her, and marched her to a chair by the bed.

She moaned, still assuming he wished to play some kind of amorous game with her. When he sat on the chair and his grasp slid to her wrist, she realised what he wanted to do. Her arousal was phenomenal and added to the thought he was about to spank her, it only made her body quiver with need. She glanced at him, in a trance. There was limited resistance when he flung her across his knees, face down.

When his first set of smacks crashed on her buttocks, she whimpered. "Marcus..."

"Before you suppose you can twist me around your little finger, we have some unfinished business." And he walloped her ass hard in two successive swats. A whimper scampered from her mouth. The harshness of his hand found her backside again and took her breath away.

"I apologised this morning!" she whined, tears forming in her eyes, but he didn't let up. Another set of slaps bounced on her creamy, fleshy butt.

She yelped.

"You did. Sure. But you must realise the enormity of your mistakes; you need to remember the lesson. Just apologizing won't do." He whacked her perfect and ravishing half globes.

"Please!" Erin begged, but his hand connected with her ass right in the middle, and the sting stilled her.

"Never behave like last night again, placing yourself and others at risk, in danger. Understood?"

"Darling," she let out in a heavy breath.

"You haven't grasped the gravity of it, my lovely. Today, you will. Promise me, you'll never act like that again." And another swat came on to her, by then, flaming red, apple cheeks.

"I promise, I swear." Tears were streaming from her eyes. The scorching on her behind was unbearable, his firm hand unleashing burning swats one after the other on her scarlet skin. It was as if she had gone to the depths of Hell, with fire blazing her ass. It would wither in the seething heat of his spanks as a rose would shrivel away in the crackling desert sun.

"No more tantrums, distrust, or dangerous plans, do you understand?" he asked as he branded her delectable rear.

It was flaming, the sting insufferable. If her pussy had been throbbing before, the deep hotness within her centre soared to stratospheric temperatures, like molten lava spreading inside her. She was aching for him with a desperate need. Her sex engorged, she needed release.

"I do…" she whimpered in desperation, "please, Marcus."

"You are forbidden to drink any alcohol, is that clear?" And he swatted her skin again, forcefully, until she was whimpering, her body limp and barely able to speak.

"I beg you…" she muttered through sobs.

"You will not drive anybody's car without my permission. Understood?"

"Yes."

She couldn't bear the stinging on her cherry-tinted bottom any longer. The more he flattened it with his hand, the more it glowed and burned. And the slick, damp hot mess between her legs, already dripping and aching for fulfilment from the sexy dancing, the fervent kissing and his teasing fingers, throbbed with want and need at his spanks. She felt humiliated at being chastised. But her desire for him was more bewildering to her.

Another wallop and she moaned in lust. Her croaky moan made him smile.

"I see, not really a punishment after all, is it?" And he stopped, putting a hand on her supple flushed ass, and rubbed. The warmth of his palm after the spanking was marvellous. She tried to contain herself from moaning any louder.

He parted her legs and placed his fingertips at her entrance. "God, you are drenched, my love. Tell me, what shall I do now, ah?" And he teased her opening, poking and playing with her slit, and when he placed his fingers in her tender, wet hotness, she rumbled a slow hiss.

"Don't come. I'm not allowing you until I say so. This is not for your gratification but a deterrent to bad behaviour."

She was too far gone. A few thrusts was all it took. She exploded so loudly with the orgasm, he thought they would hear her all the way to the clinic. He grinned with pleasure, though, her arousal making him proud, even if she had disobeyed his order.

Marcus continued to thrust inside her until her juices were drenching his fingers. He licked them. "You taste good all over, Erin, but still not listening, hey?"

The strength of her orgasm dazed her. "Ah?"

He sat her on his lap and wiped a few straggling tears on her cheeks. "You sweet poppet," he mumbled. He brushed his lips on her eyebrows.

She fluttered her eyelashes at him, overwhelmed.

It caused him to smile. He fisted her hair in his hand and kissed her generous, heavenly mouth, appeasing his hunger for her like a starving man. God, her lips were so kissable! He didn't remember enjoying kissing a woman as much as he did with Erin, not even with Penny.

She put her arms around his neck, and their mouths made a symphony of love. They couldn't have enough of each other.

"You are disobedient, poppet. What am I going to do with you? I told you not to come!" he chastised her when the kiss ended, shaking his head. But his expression was dark with passion.

"I couldn't..." she whispered. He raised an eyebrow, but she took his mouth.

"Umm... don't know if I should let this drop because you kiss this good," he said, biting playfully on her bottom lip. He lifted her in his arms and deposited her on the bed. He moved over her, caressing her skin. Then he shifted his lips to her swollen, firm, eager, pink-tipped breasts. He loved her voluptuous breasts, ample and magnificent. He captured her aching peaks, fondling them, and he sucked, stroked, and squeezed them until they tightened and peaked like pebbles.

All the while, small little cries whimpered out of her, as her nipples wobbled and throbbed inside his mouth and between his fingers. Her wetness flooded the apex of her legs soon enough. Her beads were delectable, and he enjoyed gorging on them. He flicked his finger over her swelled bosom, and she simpered her need. She was ripe for him.

He lifted his head and looked into her eyes, dazed with desire again, completely his, and he rejoiced.

"Sweet Jesus, you are gorgeous, always; but like this, you are Venus!" He scampered back. He peeked at her from on his feet, at the edge. She made as if to rise.

"Don't move; stay as you are," he said. "I wish to look at you. Lie back."

She hesitated for a moment, uncertain, but then watched him as he observed her. Her eyes intent on his, on the tiniest expressions of his face, she could swear she saw something magic in that look. Love and awe! So, she lay on the bed and let him have a fill of her.

Marcus's eyes roamed over her shapely curves to his heart's content. Capturing this moment in a glorious memory, he enjoyed getting a load of his woman's body, taking all of her in, fully aroused. Her breast and lips swollen, her ass scarlet, Erin looked thoroughly fucked then, and his cock was still waiting in the wings.

He was still wearing his trousers. He smiled at her, and she returned a coy one. Her cheeks burned at his lustful inspection of her. But she loved every second, feeling her power at this minute.

Marcus unhooked his leather belt from the loops of his trousers. But when he didn't drop it and, instead, held the buckle firmly in his palm, wrapping the leather around and fisting it, leaving the other end loose, it shocked her. Her brows shot up.

"What are you doing?" she mumbled in apprehension.

He gave her a sinful smile and whipped his other palm with the tip of the belt, testing it. "This will do," he said, looking at her with a wide grin.

"What?" She scampered backwards on her derrière, on all fours. He caught her ankle and tugged her to him to the edge of the bed. She squealed.

"My spanking was no punishment at all. You were soaked. It gave you an almighty climax! You'll misbehave again so I can make you come with my smacks. I have to deliver some kind of message you will remember. Now turn over and show your gorgeous backside to me," he said, holding her ankle, but she was shaking her leg, trying to lose his grip.

She didn't move. "I've learnt my lesson. I swear."

"My kisses have not turned you deaf, my love, have they?" He laughed, and she kicked him with her loose leg.

"My bottom is still raw with your smacks."

"I asked you not to come, but you did, without my permission. As usual, you don't listen, darling."

"I am sorry."

"Umm…" he mumbled.

She kept on thrashing and kicking him feebly, with not much conviction to it, more for show than anything. Somehow, Marcus gripping the strap aroused her, as she both dreaded it and wished it.

Suddenly, he clasped both her ankles in his hand after a brief struggle and pulled her legs up straight, high, clutching them tight.

"What are you doing?" she shrieked in a mild panic this time.

With no preamble, he lashed the tip of his leather across her reddened butt cheeks

She yelped. It was hurtful! On top of an already burning ass, she thought she was going to die.

"You need a good belting, so you won't think my spanking was just for your enjoyment, for your sexual gratification. But I'll go easy on you today, as your gorgeous backside is sore already. Five welts should do it," he said as it whipped down on her delicious rump.

She cried out and her eyes watered at the sting and burn on her butt. Her tears came down her face. She whimpered in lust this time as she felt another excruciating welt, her insides clenching. She couldn't understand how a cool piece of leather on her bottom could have this effect on her.

Her croaky moan made him smile. Two more lashes, and he dropped the belt on the floor. He rubbed her buttocks with his palm for a while and she moaned louder in both pain and desire, half in arousal and half in agony. He then took one of her ankles in each hand and parted her legs, nestling himself between them. Her derrière was on fire from the smacking and the belt. Thank God, at the least, the belting was only five! They had set her ass ablaze, but the ardent heat inside her fired to a smouldering temperature. She would have laughed if someone had told her a belting and a spanking would soar her arousal to Heaven, but it had, despite her searing, crimson butt.

He leaned on her and caressed her face. "Are you going to listen to me, darling? Ha? Behave as a grown-up woman rather than a brat? Umm…"

"Yes, I promise," she simpered, and their eyes locked. His lips delved on hers with a feverish exchange, bewitching her as his tongue pillaged inside her mouth, dancing and sparring with hers. They kissed, long and hard. Marcus caressed her hair when the kiss ended. He drew back and stood by the side of the bed. He took his trousers and boxers off as she watched him in anticipation, still panting from his fervent kisses.

As he placed one of her legs on each side of his shoulders, his manhood strained in full glory. He parted her soft folds, and when he slammed his erection into her, a rush of blood pumped in her body.

She cried out with ecstasy.

"Don't come until I tell you," he said. And this time she obeyed, as his cock swelled and throbbed in her wet deliciousness.

"Oooh…" she mumbled.

"Gorgeous and tight! God, I love fucking you!" He pumped her hard.

She tried to contain herself as his iron-rod lunged inside her, while her striped buttocks burned where his hips thumped into her backside. The combination of her sore bottom and Marcus riding her with his steely bulge sent her into a delirium. When he finally gave her permission to come, her ecstasy erupted strong and fast. He wasn't long behind her, and his hot seed spilled in her pulsating channel. He crashed and tangled with her in satiated pleasure on top of her.

Marcus brushed his lips on hers in a lingering, delicate kiss. Tender endearments purred out of his mouth in a silvery, mellow tone, enchanting her. He delighted her, not only with the sweet words, but the bass voice made her body tingle and shiver in the aftermath of their lovemaking, as if he were singing to her his love song.

He withdrew from her and rolled onto the side, pulling her with him in a close embrace.

They stayed silent, entwined in the warmth of their bodies for some time. Then they repeated their lovemaking until they fell asleep in each other's arms.

Chapter 16

He awakened two hours later. Erin was huddled up to him, cocooned in his arms, her back to him, her legs entangled with his. The bedsheets and coverlet were rumpled and half on the floor. What a wonderful way to wake up. A satiated smile curled up on his face as his mind registered the scene and flashed back to their lovemaking frolics from earlier on. He had missed this; he shifted closer to her and clasped her tighter to him. A lavender waft hit his nostrils. He loved the scent of her skin and would breathe her in all day. Marcus could smell her on himself too, and he inhaled, contented.

He lay there for a few minutes, relishing her closeness. He held onto her tightly as if someone was about to take her away. Closing his eyes, he savoured the thrilling moment. When he opened them, he reached out to pull her hair from her face to watch her. She had a radiant glow about her. He skimmed a fingertip on her cheek and marvelled at her beauty. His breath quickened, and the tingling sensation in his nether regions raised his temperature.

Could life be this good again for me? He hoped so. His heart was thumping fast. The singsong it let out in the air was clear to him. It said, *you have found your mate for life.* And it was Erin, lying next to him. He released a satisfied sigh, then reared his head to glance at the clock. Damn! It was two pm.

He would like nothing better than to ravish her, to plunge inside her again. But he had to make a move. He had too much to do. Half of his day had gone already. Even as pleasant as it had been, she would have to wait. Perhaps later, he could resume where they had left off.

He needed to look in on Goran, to see how he was doing. Besides, Erin required new clothes. He scoffed at the image of him throwing her bags out of the car last night. Incredible! He smiled.

Go on, man, get up!

He tried to disentangle himself from her without waking her up, which was not a mean feat. Every time he untangled one limb, she moved to tangle herself, faster, with another. He laughed, caressed her hair back and kissed her forehead.

Reluctantly, he finally disentangled himself. He covered her with the blanket and tacked her in, as if she were a precious baby. *Oh, yes! She is my baby, my woman.* For a mature fellow, he chuckled at the nonsense in his mind. *For heaven's sake, man, snap up, you are forty-one!* But his soul felt lighter than it had in years.

He put on his boxers, jeans, and a t-shirt and went downstairs to the kitchen for a drink. Marcus opened the fridge to see what he had, taking out a can of cola.

When he closed the door, he almost jumped out of his skin. "Jesus, Winnie!" he cried out. "You made me jump. What the hell are you doing here?"

"Oh, I beg your pardon, Doctor. Good afternoon. Dr. Devlin knocked at the front door, but there was no reply. She let me in, thought you may be hungry. I brought you lunch," the cook replied, pointing at the tray of goodies on the table. "Just now, I was replacing the biscuits in your study, sir."

"Thank you," he said through gritted teeth. He was not happy with his sister.

Let the woman in like that? Bloody Hell! What if he or Erin were naked and... Julia could be careless sometimes. He'd have to have a word with her on this.

"There is lunch for two on the tray. Miss Blake is still here, isn't she?" Winnie said, lifting an eyebrow. She looked about her with a mischievous smile on her face.

"Well... no, she spent the night at my sister's and—"

His cook ignored his statement and drew her brows in with thin lips at what was a clear white lie. "Tell her I put her clothes in the dryer, Doctor. The washing machine cycle finished, and they needed drying. They are in the utility room, ready." The woman added with a grin, "This morning, good job it was just me in the kitchen, sir. She had a coat on, but I saw—"

"All right, Winnie, that's all, thank you," he said petulantly with a sigh. He hadn't blushed since the fourth grade, but for a second a flush crept up his neck, and the woman's eyes were glinting with mischief and a certain pride.

The cook was very fond of him. The woman mumbled her goodbye and left.

Marcus had to admit he was famished. Being a big man, he ate copious amounts of food, and all that lovemaking had made him ravenous. The delicious smell from the tray was making his mouth water.

He went back upstairs. "Darling, wake up!" He kissed her forehead, but she turned the other way without a sound.

"Hey, sweetheart, come on, up you go." He patted her backside when it was clear she had no intention of getting up. But she shuffled onto the far side, away from him, taking the blanket with her.

He laughed, got up and walked around the bed. He sat next to her again. Marcus caressed her face and kissed her hair. "Erin, my love, wake up. Time to get up."

She shifted and wrapped herself loosely in the coverlet like a mummy. She slithered along to the other side of the bed, away from him.

He roared with laughter and walked back to her side, undeterred. "Come on, poppet!" He dragged a hand through his hair and chuckled. She was about to roll and switch sides again when he put his arm around her midriff and grabbed her. He stopped her from moving any farther, keeping her tight in his hold. "Hey, sleepyhead, come on, time to get up. Lunch is ready, before it gets cold."

"Umm… no. I want to sleep," she mumbled with a small pout.

His eyes danced at her, he gave her a kiss, and she replied to him in kind. She pulled one arm out of the coverlet, draping it around his neck voluptuously, and drew him to her for a deeper kiss. He chortled but reacted to her passionate kiss.

"You are gorgeous and sexy, Dr. Stewart. Has anyone told you that?" she mumbled with hooded eyes when the kiss ended.

He scoffed and caressed her lips with his thumb. "Come on; up you go."

"Why can't we stay in bed?"

"As much as I would love to stay in bed with you, darling, I must have food. You need new clothes, and I must check on Goran. So up, please." He swatted her backside hard, getting a response from her.

"Aw, aw." She sat up.

"Hurry and put something on. Lunch will get cold, and I am starving. Move, poppet." He left with a wink. If he'd stayed when she got up, her gloriously naked body would have been too much of a temptation. He went downstairs on the double before she could lure him into bed again.

"God, it smells delicious! Did you do this?" she asked, when she joined him in the kitchen wearing his shirt and leaned in to smell the food.

"I am a man of many talents, darling," he replied with a wink, "but this is out of my league. Winnie brought us lunch, and she almost gave me a heart attack. My sister let her in, unannounced."

"Unannounced? Oh, what if we…" And she waved her hand between the two of them with her eyes wide in horror.

"My sentiments exactly!"

"Does she know I am here?"

"Didn't you say they are taking bets? Besides, Winnie found your clothes in the washing machine and moved them to the dryer. All bets may come in thick and fast now, I can assure you."

"Oh, we are done and dusted, then. Your reputation, Dr. Stewart, as an upstanding citizen, is in tatters. No redemption. Everyone will think you are a playboy, or worse, a man-whore!" She giggled. She wouldn't deny her happiness that their relationship was out in the open. Their secret was out, and she couldn't care less who knew it. Or what anybody said.

"Man-whore?" He arched a brow, and she schooled her features, pretending to be serious again. But he went on, "You are right. Gossip will be rife and rumours will escalate."

"It's not that bad, darling. We are both single people, consenting adults, and we are not harming anyone." She smiled, but he rolled his eyes.

"Let's not worry about this now," Marcus huffed with a minor irritation. "After lunch, I'll need to look in on Goran." He wouldn't think about this. He hated gossip above all, even worse if he was the subject of it. Though she was right; they were consenting adults. Anyhow, there was no point in crying over spilt milk. The cat was out of the bag, namely, their love for one another, and there was nothing they could do. He sighed. What the hell, eventually it would have happened, anyway.

"I'll come with you to look in on Goran, after lunch."

"No, you won't."

"Darling, I must see him, I must apologise."

"And you will, but not today. Leave him alone. He is resting," he commanded.

"Marcus——" she insisted. He came closer to her and kissed her, silencing her. A peremptory kiss that told her discussion closed on that matter.

"I said no. No more arguments, please. While I am gone, get ready. We must go into town; you need clothes."

"Fine!" she mumbled reluctantly. "But where the hell are my bags, I wonder…" And she gave him a suspicious glance.

"Okay, guilty! I threw them out of the car last night during our little, ahem… excursion… but I'll buy you new ones," he admitted with a laugh.

"I knew it!"

After lunch, he had a shower. He almost called out to Erin to join him but thought better of it. He was in a hurry, and having her in the shower… *Well, maybe later,* he promised himself.

He was ready in no time.

———

"I'LL BE BACK in an hour, then we will go into town," he said and kissed her.

Before he left, she stopped him. "Take this to him." She gave him an envelope.

"What's this?"

"An apology to Goran. I'll apologise in person, too. If you won't let me see him, this note will have to do for now," she replied, lowering her eyes.

"Don't worry; I'll tell him." He nodded, took the envelope, and went to the clinic.

Good God, the damn letters! How could I be so stupid, Jesus!

Giving him the note for Goran, reminded her of the other letters she had written and left in Marcus's office at the clinic the previous night. The original plan was for him to find them after Erin had gone. Her plot failed, and the outcome changed. There was no need for them anymore. But with the subsequent hubbub of the night, the letters had slipped her mind.

She had forgotten all about them. Marcus had mentioned nothing about this. More than likely, he had not seen them yet.

Erin worried about one particular letter, the one she had written to him, spilling out all her feelings for him. She had poured her heart out without reservations in that letter, and she didn't want him to read it.

It would have been different if he read it when she had gone out of his life forever. As it was, she was still there. He should not read this letter now, not in the present circumstances. The strength of her passion for him might put him off, scare him. It was too soon. She would feel embarrassed and exposed.

She had to retrieve the letters and dispose of them.

Chapter 17

S he showered and dressed at the speed of light, then she made her way to the clinic. She ran into Belinda in the gardens.

"Hey, where have you been? Or do I guess?" Her friend had a playful smile, her eyes bright and dancing with curiosity. She stared at her with that knowing look.

"No need," Erin said flatly, turning her gaze away. Her cheeks burned like a log on fire.

"Oh, come on, Erin. What is that I hear? Is it true?" her companion asked. "You and Dr. Stewart? Everyone is talking about it. I've been saying it for months... I knew it!"

"Oh, God!" She rolled her eyes, and her pace quickened as if she craved to run away.

"Oh, no! Don't give me the silent treatment now that you have a juicy thing to tell me. Go on; spill it!"

"Bella!" Erin said in a warning tone, giving her a scowl. Though she couldn't help herself, and a small smile formed on her lips.

"Oh, you dark horse! Don't worry. I always knew you would end up in his bed. I would like to say, your secret is safe with me… but, darling, it's no secret. Good on you. You landed the unobtainable doctor, then. Not sure how this spread so fast, but you'll have to tell me all. Do not leave a word out!"

"Belinda, please, not now… I'm in a hurry." Though she was somehow pleased Belinda was teasing her about it, nonetheless, Erin had to agree. Marcus had been right all along to keep their relationship private. For the same reason, she felt uncomfortable talking about it now, fresh out of his bed. He was aware from the outset that this would happen. And it had, but it was all academic now.

She scoffed. "And you missed Goran having a turn. Poor lamb! Oh, don't upset yourself, he is fine now. He is in the emergency room, just as a precaution. Not sure what's wrong with him."

"Jesus!" Erin felt distressed at deceiving her friend on this issue, but there was already too much talk. She couldn't tell her. She would not add fuel to it. Besides, she felt too ashamed to talk about it.

"Lily was distraught when she found out Goran was ill. She became hysterical. They took her in to see him for a few minutes before she had a heart attack herself. God, those two. I'll have to buy a hat soon; I feel a wedding is in the air." She laughed. "Lily said he looks fine. A little pale, and he has a sore throat, but he is okay."

"Does he know what happened?"

"No. He is feeling better, but Lily was impossible until she saw him."

"Sweet Lord!"

"It's not like you to miss all the action. Well, if I was in a handsome man's bed, with some action of my own, I would not be paying attention to anything else, either," Belinda said with a breezy laugh.

"Oh, drop it."

"Don't be such a mope! You can't deny there was a lot of excitement last night." She smirked, lifting her brows.

"Perhaps, there is a bit more action, Bella. I need a favour."

They kept on walking towards the clinic at a pace.

"What is it? And why are you marching like a trooper! I can't keep up, with my stilettos."

"One of these days, Belinda, you'll break your neck when you fall off the great height of your stilettos."

"Hey, I enjoy wearing them. I can run a fifty-meter race on these as if I were on Nike trainers, I'll have you know. Anyway, what is it you want?"

"You need to distract Nurse Stevenson for me. I must go into Dr. Stewart's office." Erin glanced at her friend who was watching her, puzzled.

Her companion scowled, a tad worried. "Dr. Stewart? Why?"

"I have to fetch something in it."

"What?"

"Are you going to help me or not? If you are, do not ask questions. And hurry before he goes back to his office. It may be too late, anyway."

"No, Dr. Stewart is with Goran."

"I see. Then, we must hurry."

"I take it you don't have permission to go in there."

"Are you game, Belinda? Yes, or no?" Erin increased her pace, and Belinda followed at a trot.

"I am always game, darling! What shall I do?"

"Then, now is the time to run the fifty-meter race on your high heels. Move!"

"MISS WALTHAM," Nurse Stevenson said. "What can I do for you?"

"Is Dr. Stewart in his office?"

"No, the doctor has not been in there today."

"Dr. Devlin is looking for you. She wants you in the emergency room right away. She needs you and Dr. Stewart there," Belinda said nonchalantly. A sweet smile plastered her angel's face, expressing innocence.

"I thought he was already in there."

"Oh, I don't know about that. Devlin said you should join her there."

"Me? Are you sure?" The nurse shifted in her chair, looking uncertain.

"Aha."

"And hurry. It is urgent."

"Of course!" The nurse rose from her desk and left in a haste.

Belinda had a quick glance about her. There was nobody around. She knocked on Dr. Stewart's office door just in case, though she knew he wasn't there. When there was no reply, she made her way swiftly into the room. She headed towards the French doors. She opened them to let Erin in from the garden.

"Stevenson is gone. It won't be long before she is back when she discovers it's a lie."

"Go to the door. Stand guard and warn me if anyone is coming." Erin was nervous, and she gulped. Her friend nodded and moved fast out of the room to stand outside.

Erin went to his desk but couldn't remember in which drawer she had placed the letters. She'd had a few glasses of wine by then, last night, so her recollection was a little blurred. She had to open them all. Besides, she had hidden them under other things in the drawer. She had to rummage through them, too.

Success at last, she found them. She was done. She pulled them out and made her way out of the room to where Belinda stood. As she opened the door, her companion collided with her under the doorframe on her way in.

"Jesus. You almost head butted me!"

"He's coming. Hide!" Belinda cried out, and Erin had a quick glance at the hallway. Marcus's purposeful and powerful strides, with the nurse in tow, were heading in her direction.

She gulped.

"Bloody hell! The garden doors, run!" Precious seconds were lost as they jostled with one another trying to get into the room first, at the same time. They ran towards the French doors, to make their escape, but it was a few moments too late.

"Stop right there!" he boomed at them from the doorframe, a thunderous expression on his face.

The girls froze as they were about to step out into the garden. Their gazes spanned to him, and Erin swallowed a lump in her throat. She held her hand with the letters behind her back, hiding them, as Marcus and his assistant walked into the office.

"Miss Waltham told me to go to the emergency room," the nurse mumbled, her pretty face in a scowl.

"Well, perhaps I was mistaken. Uh… maybe Dr. Devlin said to ask Matron. I got confused," Belinda blabbered in her defence.

Stevenson's frown deepened. "I don't think so," she said, irritation written all over her face.

"That's okay. I'll handle this. You can go," he said to Stevenson. When she tried to rebuke, one look at her and he shut her up.

"Yes, Doctor." The girl retreated, closing the door behind herself.

"What the hell are you two doing in my office?" he asked, a dark expression on his face, arms akimbo.

The girls glanced at each other and blushed. Their shoulders slumped at being caught in the act.

Marcus lifted his eyebrows and huffed, discontented. "I'm waiting, and don't make me ask you again. What the hell is this about?"

"Well, w-we..." Belinda began and shuffled, looking at Erin then at the doctor.

"I have a very short fuse today, so don't waste my time, or it will end up in tears."

"I'm sorry, Marcus, it's my fault. She has nothing to do with this. She was just on the lookout. My apologies. She's not to blame."

"True!" Belinda whimpered, seeing his dark countenance.

"You, out!" he bellowed at her, gesturing to the door with his thumb over his shoulder, "and, Belinda, if I catch you in my office again without permission, Fergus will hear about it. Understood?"

"Yes. Sorry, Doctor."

"Now, out!" he cried out. The girl scampered out of the room with a sympathetic smile to her friend.

Erin's eyes darted from her companion's swift exit to Marcus, and the dim look on his face said it all.

"What the hell is this, Erin? God, you are exasperating. Did you listen to nothing I said this morning about your behaviour, hey?"

"Well, I-I—"

"Show me what you've got behind your back!"

"N-nothing—"

"Erin!" he boomed, and it made her jump on the spot. "I had enough of your antics yesterday to last me a lifetime. So, let's not start again. Give it to me!"

"Marcus..." He went to her, but she moved away.

She scurried along to the opposite side, circling his desk, and ran to the fireplace. With the remnants of a fire smouldering, she threw the letters into the fire.

He cursed and gave her a dirty look. Then, he got hold of a fire poker and retrieved them, while she tried to impede him, getting in his way. He stopped her from advancing near them, pushing her away with his outstretched arm, as he thumped on the scorched papers on the floor.

He trampled out a tiny flame on the edge of the letters with his heavy boots. Then he spun to her with a fierce expression. "You try one more thing, and I won't be responsible for your backside today. Understood? Stand still and stop this nonsense."

"They are mine. I wrote them before I tried to leave, to apologise to people for doing it. They are personal, and you shouldn't read them. I want to burn them." She pouted like an uncooperative child and stomped her foot on the floor.

He picked them up. They were scorched at one corner but otherwise readable. He glanced at them. There was a letter for Zac, another for Finley, one for Goran, and the last was addressed to himself. It dawned on him what was going on. She had written a letter to him and now she was trying to destroy it. He became curious about it and above everything in the world, he wanted to read it.

Marcus took the ones addressed to the others and threw them back into the fire, to her great relief. She sighed. When she realised he had saved one, it did not take rocket science to guess which one he had kept. Her face blanched.

Marcus saw the colour draining from her face as she stared desperately at his hand.

"Burn that letter too!"

"That's why you are here! No? I presume you left it in my office, and now you were stealing it."

"Stealing it?" she cried out and scowled at him.

"You addressed this one to me. It's mine, and I read all my letters." He grinned with mischief, which irritated the hell out of her.

"No! Please. Give it to me." She launched herself at him, demanding it, wanting to seize the letter.

He laughed and stood back, towering over her, imposing. Though Erin was a tall lady, Marcus was a few inches taller. He lifted his arm up in the air, with the letter in his hand, out of her reach. It became inaccessible to her as she was struggling to grab it from him, with tiny little jumps. She thundered a few curses at him.

"What's in it, poppet, hey?" He chuckled. "Will I like what I read, or did you write a list of curses at me. Which is it?" His grin was becoming wider and more mischievous as her whole demeanour told him how worried she was. He lifted his eyes to his palm and smiled, while with his other hand, he grabbed her wrist, pulling it behind her back as his arm encircled her waist tight, immobilising her somewhat.

"Stop now, before I lose my patience." This time his voice was harsh and commanding.

Her chin quivered. "Give me my letter! Please. I beg you." She bit her lip, with her free hand tugging at his arm, still outstretched high above her, out of reach.

"No."

"Marcus…" She stomped her foot repeatedly.

"God, Erin, you are thirty-three behaving like a three-year-old!"

"It is mine; give it to me!"

"No, you addressed it to me. And now it belongs to me." He chuckled and was relishing the tittle-tattle with his woman.

Erin blushed furiously as he made fun of her. He put the letter in his mouth and held both of her wrists as he backed her against his desk. Then he spun her over, forcing her to bend on the counter, face down.

She struggled and complained, but she was no match for his strength. He smacked her rump over her clothes, three or four times, hard, until she quieted with his painful swats.

"Aw, aw," she expressed her dissatisfaction at him in no uncertain terms, but one last mighty wallop took her breath away. Her backside still tender from the morning spanking and belting, it didn't take long to calm down, with her buttocks on fire. She would not be sitting comfortably for a while after the series of spankings she'd suffered at his solid hand. She could feel her rear end sizzling. Her sore arse would be a reminder to her of her shenanigans and his firm, powerful spankings for days.

He stopped and rubbed her buttocks for a few seconds, still with a smirk on his face. Then he released her and took the letter out of his mouth.

She rose and rubbed her backside in agony. A pinched mouth and a sour expression marred her face.

"Sit!" He pointed at the chair, his feet in a wide stance, daring her to defy him again. Not to mention, the clenched jaw and crease in his brows told her she would not win this battle.

She decided it was best to get it over with. He was determined to read it.

"Do you mind if I stand? Sitting is a little sore right now," she simpered.

He chuckled. "Okay, but I want no interruptions as I read it, understood?"

Erin nodded and exhaled. She stood there as quiet as a mouse, but she launched a frown at him and crossed her arms on her chest.

He went behind his desk and sat in his chair. A small smile on his lips, he opened the letter and read.

"MY DEAREST MARCUS,

It has taken me several attempts to put down on paper these few lines.

As you read this letter, it means I have left the clinic of my own free will. Well, the thing is… I ran away.

Forgive me for being so underhanded in doing this, but I had no choice.

It was regrettable it had to end this way. I enjoyed my time at the clinic.

But you lied to me. I know about you and Nurse Stevenson, but no matter. I forgive you all the same.

My forgiveness comes from the soul, without bitterness, because I love you with all my heart and I want you to be happy. I am not resentful.

Your happiness is important to me, even if it does not include me. Though I'll never love again like I do now.

Be happy with her. I can't say if she worships you like I do, but if she does half as much as I do, she loves you very much indeed.

It'll suck without you and without my friends, especially without you, but I'll be brave.

Do not worry about me. I have survived worse things in my life, I'll survive this too.

Besides, the passion we shared, even if short-lived, has warmed me up and I'll take it with me.

My temperature rises thinking about you... on me... God, I'd better stop this line of thought before I get too hot!

Anyway, in the last few weeks, I have had a dream. A recurrent one, of a day at the regatta. Your face is there. It is always loving to me, and then it scowls. I wonder why you scowl at me in my dream at the regatta, perhaps to tell me you love her and not me?

Who knows? I'll bet Dr. Devlin would have an answer for it, but I am too shy to ask. But I digress.

Your sister helped me to exorcise the demons of my past, and for that I will be eternally grateful to her and to my time at the clinic.

You have nurtured me in our brief relationship and made me whole again. That night at the hotel was the happiest of my life. I believe in possibilities now. Even if this one didn't work out, some other will! I know it in my heart, and for this, I thank you. Though I'll never love another man like I love you.

Oh, don't get me wrong, my brain wants to shout improprieties at you for lying to me and slap your damn handsome face! I cried for the last three days because of you. You big oaf!

I am writing the letter out of the emotions I feel for you, from my heart. Despite everything, I wish you the best, and if your best is with Stevenson, then so be it.

It may take some time for me to forget you, but I am a survivor, and I will endure it.

Please forgive me if my disappearance will bring you problems.

Be happy!

Yours forever.

Erin"

MARCUS TOOK ages in reading the letter. Erin guessed he had read it at least twice. She fiddled with her necklace, twirling it around her neck. She was as white as a ghost. Her chest felt constricted; she couldn't breathe. Her stomach was in knots, trying to second guess what he was thinking. Her confidence was faltering. She finally plopped on the chair, as her knees were wobbling, burning arse and all. She clasped her knees tightly with her hands to avoid them from trembling.

She was on tenterhooks. Erin fidgeted, as if the chair was on fire. A bit was because of her glowing, scorching backside. Mostly, as his eyes scanned her intimate letter, she felt as if she was walking on hot stones. *Jesus, how long does it take for him to read the bloody thing?* She couldn't bear the wait.

What had possessed her to write the stupid letter, she couldn't tell. She was an idiot. God knows what he was thinking. As he read it, Erin focused on his face, scrutinising every tiny movement. She saw him smile twice, with amusement in his eyes once, then deep concentration, consternation, and that scowl again. The same one as in her dream! An array of emotions were going through his face.

She was on the edge of her seat. Those minutes seemed to her like hours. His eyes had that rapt attention on the letter, as if he didn't want to miss a single word on it, trying to absorb all she written in it.

God help her! After the lovely morning they'd had, now this! She always ruined everything.

"Well?" she asked at last. She succumbed to her impatience, not being able to wait as he folded the piece of paper carefully back in the envelope.

"You are a sweet poppet!" he said and laughed. His eyes were dancing with a variety of emotions she could not describe.

"What the hell does that mean?" She rose abruptly from her chair, shuffling on her feet. Then she plopped down on the chair again, disheartened.

"Come; we need to get you some clothes before the shops close. We are late. You cannot go around the estate in my shirt, as much as I adore you in it." He got up from behind his desk and came 'round to her. He pulled her out of the chair.

"Marcus, you are irritating and—-" she ventured, but he silenced her.

He wrapped his arms around her waist and drew her to him. She looked into his eyes, searching, wondering, and he crushed his mouth to hers. He ravished her with his kiss, leaving her breathless, panting, and dazed.

"No time to waste. They are waiting for us at the store; let's go," he said when the kiss ended. They left, using his sister's car to go into town.

She was puzzled, not knowing what to think. He hadn't made a single comment about it. Why? Did he like the letter? Or did he feel it was stupid? More likely, the latter, she sensed. Did her passion scare him? Did she come on too strong?

They drove in silence. She was too embarrassed to say a word. When they arrived and he parked the car, he turned to her, his eyes dancing with mirth.

"You know, with all this rifling gossip, I'll have to make an honest woman out of you," he said with amusement.

"What? You mean…" Her eyes were big and round, as she struggled to compute his words.

"You heard me."

"Do you mean what I think you mean?"

"I do!" he said, and her eyes gleamed like stars. A wide smile spread on her face. But he went on, "But save your answer for when I have a ring for you, poppet."

"You are awfully sure of yourself," she said, lifting her brows.

He leaned over and kissed the tip of her nose, caressing her face, then he grinned at her. "Aren't you?"

"Oh, Marcus, I-I—"

"And about your dream at the regatta, Erin, you don't need Julia to tell you what it means. I can tell you."

"You can? What is it, then?"

"That's where we first met, Erin, at the regatta, fourteen years ago. Your subconscious knows. Your dream is trying to say this to you… willing you to remember our first encounter."

"Really? We did?"

"I took one look at you, then, and I have loved you ever since."

Chapter 18

They married three weeks later. She wondered why the hurry, though she didn't mind it.

"Shouldn't we get to know each better first?"

"Do you have any doubts, poppet?" Marcus asked, his eyes intent on her, searching hers.

"Me? No, darling, I've never been so sure of anything in my life. I worship you, and I'm spoiling you with my love, way too much."

"Well, you carry on spoiling me, then. I have waited fourteen years, Erin. I won't wait any longer. Besides, you may have some other silly ideas of yours... I can keep an eye on you like this, as my wife." He gazed at her, a hint of amusement in his tone. She returned her best smile, and he kissed her.

"Ooh..." she mumbled when the kiss ended.

"I must make an honest woman out of you, anyway. Too much gossip," he said with an amused expression. She burst out laughing.

They got married in the small medieval chapel in the village. Goran gave the bride away, while Zac was Marcus's best man.

Belinda was Erin's maid of honour. As she couldn't decide who to choose, so Lily, Julia, Clara, Mollie and Kathryn were all her bridesmaids, the girls enjoying the attention.

The small congregation made their way back to a private room at the clinic to celebrate. Winnie had surpassed herself and prepared a banquet for the guests.

They later cut the cake in the main dining room, where patients and staff joined them too. Even the young police officer, Tom, had attended the celebration.

"You won't drive today, Mrs. Stewart? I know how you like your speed when you drink," the officer whispered in jest.

She smiled at him, thinking if he had arrested her, perhaps her life would have turned out somewhat different. "Bless you, Tom, no, I won't!"

She looked resplendent on her wedding day in a simple but elegant white lace dress, and she could not contain her joy. They ate, they danced, and they shared their bliss in the company of friends. It was a marvellous day. After the misery of the past year, there was light at the end of the tunnel for her. She realised that with him at her side, she would withstand any curve ball life threw at her.

It was eight months later, the following June, when Marcus could take time off for the long-awaited honeymoon. They cruised the Italian Lakes, where the waters shimmered in assorted shades of blue. They stopped at unspoiled villages on the shore where the world revolved at a quieter pace. While connecting the lakes, they traveled to fine cities in the country. Stylish Milan, where they gazed at the Duomo Cathedral and admired the Da Vinci's Last Supper. They visited Verona, a charming city where they dropped by to see Juliette's house. They knew that the fictional character from Shakespeare's play in "Romeo and Juliette" never lived there. But it had never stopped people from traveling there. So, it didn't stop them, either.

It sounded absurd to her. She overflowed with emotion when Marcus had written a message of his love for her on the vast wall in the courtyard where thousands of amorous notes were pasted all over in Juliette's home. At least, until the surface would be washed again. His caption in the mysterious and fascinating book in the house would last forever.

"I now secured our bond for eternity. The essence of our love will be guarded in this temple of love, always," he mumbled with half a smile, amazed at the tender side of himself that had sprung from nowhere and surprised even him. A picture on the splendid balcony completed the memory.

Her eyes glistened at his romantic gestures.

That same evening, he dazzled her with a night at the opera, at the famous Arena of Verona amphitheatre. In the candlelit ancient arena, they sat on its stone steps under the stars, to the heavenly music of Giacomo Puccini's Madame Butterfly. She had never been at the opera before and didn't know what to expect.

Erin cried to Cio-Cio-San's heartfelt aria "One Fine Day" as the performance went on, while Marcus held her hand tight and whispered in her ear, "You sweet poppet."

It was okay.

That night, a magnificent starry night, in the city of Romeo and Juliette, with a scented, flowery breeze intoxicating her senses, love was king. It felt good to cry, and with Puccini's celestial music caressing her ears, the floodgates opened. She was full of emotion, and she cried buckets. She couldn't help it.

It was fine.

No one batted an eyelid, as if to say *this is how you should feel love in this place, in every pore of your being and to the depths of your soul.*

He clasped her hand throughout the performance, as if to suggest, *I'll never leave you, my darling, I will cherish you and protect you forever.*

From Verona and farther east, they sailed through the lagoons and canals of magnificent Venice, visiting the myriad of Gothic and Renaissance palaces, squares, and churches. Then, they turned back to the west of the country by train, crossing in the calmest waters of Lake Como, which Erin proclaimed, "the prettiest she had ever seen."

They traveled to Lugano in Switzerland, a stone's throw from the Italian border, on a bus ride from the village of Menaggio on the lake. It trekked across the Italian to the Swiss Alps then descended into the Swiss city.

This meant Marcus, as big as he was, sat crumpled for almost two hours on a small bus seat. The view from the top of the Alps of the huge lakes on either sides of the mountains, Lake Como and Lake Lugano, made it memorable and worth the less-than-ideal traveling conditions.

They tried their hand at kite surfing on the Northern shores of Lake Garda. They visited Sirmione and stayed by the lakeside, with two midnight dips in the freezing water that had their bodies tingling well after the dip, not to mention the want and desire satisfied afterwards.

In Lake Maggiore, they hopped between the flowery islands in the middle of this large stretch of water with a blend of harmonious colour, scent, and beautiful design.

He gave her a honeymoon to remember. It was magical.

When they returned home, she had already settled well in the cottage before their departure, so she embraced her new life. Spankings still came along on occasion, when she got a little too agitated or stubborn about something. Though, if she had to admit, she didn't mind it one bit; she loved them. It made their lovemaking that much more exciting and exhilarating. She couldn't believe how she liked his firm hand on her backside.

Soon after they returned from the honeymoon, she revealed that she was expecting their first child, to the incredible delight of all and not only Erin and Marcus.

He got so fussy around her, it was comical. It was then, she realised, all her past struggles, her suffering agony, her depression, her ups and downs, had led her to him, to this wonderful man, now her husband, and to a loving family with him. Her faith flickered in her soul, and she sent a joyful prayer to Heaven, thanking God for bringing Marcus into her life.

Raffaella Rowell

Raffaella was born in Italy and grew up in South America. She moved to England in her mid-twenties, where she currently resides. She is married and has two sons.

She has a university degree in Modern Languages and Literature. She loves a book in any genre, reads anything and every day, with a weakness for crime/thrillers, romance novels, classics and historical figures.

Raffaella writes romance novels with a twist of suspense, spicy and sexy in the midst. She also enjoys gardening, baking (legendary for her delicious baked cheesecake), and playing the piano.

Email: raffabellano@gmail.com
Instagram account: @raffaellarowell
Twitter account: @Raffaella Rowell - Author
facebook: www.facebook.com/raffaellarowell
Visit her website here:
www.raffaellarowell.com

Don't miss these exciting titles by Raffaella Rowell and Blushing Books!

The Siblings Series
A Matter of Wife and Wealth

The Trouble with Molly series
The Perfect Pairing

The Trouble with Mollie
A Creature of Spirit

Single Titles
Ice, Spice and Red Lace

Blushing Books Newsletter

Please join the Blushing Books newsletter
to receive updates & special promotional offers.
You can also join by using your mobile phone:
Just text BLUSHING to 22828.

Blushing Books

Blushing Books is one of the oldest eBook publishers on the web. We've been running websites that publish spanking and BDSM related romance and erotica since 1999, and we have been selling eBooks since 2003. We hope you'll check out our hundreds of offerings at http://www.blushingbooks.com.